BLAZING RATTLES (BOOK 10)

A HARLEY AND DAVIDSON MYSTERY

LILIANA HART

LOUIS SCOTT

To our French Bulldog, Bacon - Your love of snacks and snuggles helped us write this book. But you're going on a diet soon.

.

The Harley and Davidson Mystery Series
The Farmer's Slaughter
A Tisket a Casket
I Saw Mommy Killing Santa Claus
Get Your Murder Running
Deceased and Desist
Malice in Wonderland
Tequila Mockingbird
Gone With the Sin

CHAPTER ONE

Tuesday, February 14th

Today was the day Hank Davidson's life would change forever.

He'd thought about it, worried about it, talked about it, considered it, and reconsidered it. Finally, he'd made the decision to propose to Agatha Harley. And he was almost sure he could do it without making a fool of himself.

It had been almost three years since he'd moved to Rusty Gun, Texas. He'd spent his career as an FBI-trained serial-killer hunter, but his heart had no longer been in it, and he'd turned in his gun and badge for the lazy days of retirement.

It had been Sheriff Reggie Coil, his long-time friend, who'd first invited Hank to Rusty Gun so he could disappear and get some much needed R&R. Never in a million years had the big city murder cop thought he'd become a permanent citizen of the sleepy, southern town. Much less fall in love there.

Agatha was his perfect match. She'd once had dreams of solving high-profile criminal cases as a forensic anthropologist, but a stalker had changed the course of her life and sent her back to Rusty Gun. She'd persevered through more than he could imagine and still managed to become a successful author, writing about the very crimes she first dreamt of solving.

Agatha enjoyed small town living and was content to spend her days reading, researching and writing about the career she no longer pursued. Hank had changed all of that when the two clashed while investigating their first cold case together.

Their relationship was what some might call a slow simmer, but Hank was methodical in every aspect of his life. It's what made him one of the best homicide detectives in the world. It was what also caused him to wait months to propose while he planned everything down to the most minute detail.

To say he planned it without help would be a lie. Preparations for solving a crime were a lot different from preparations for romance. He wasn't afraid to admit his skills in romance were...lacking. He didn't understand why people couldn't just make a decision to get married and do it, but in his experience, women tended to disapprove of the cut and dried technique. And more importantly, he wanted to make it special for Agatha.

For that, he'd had to get Agatha's best friend, Heather Cartwright, involved. He and Heather had never seen eye to eye on anything, and she was one of Hank's least favorite people on the planet, but they both loved Agatha and had her best interests at heart.

Heather's favorite pastime was marriage and divorce, so she knew a thing or two about romantic proposals. She'd also accumulated a lot of wealth during her marriages, so she knew all the best places to stay and eat.

Which is why Hank had booked adjoining suites at a luxury hotel on the Riverwalk in San Antonio, a private driver, and reservations for a seven course dinner for Valentine's Day, where he'd eventually get down on one knee and pop the question. Just the thought had him breaking out in a sweat.

Hank patted the ring box in his pocket that he'd been carrying around for several days. He was afraid to let it out of his sight. He'd driven to Austin and picked it out himself, finding a unique design that reminded him of Agatha—because she was definitely unique in every way.

He knew his mind should be on the upcoming weekend getaway, but he couldn't help but be distracted by the email he'd gotten from the FBI field office in Philadelphia—his old stomping ground. He needed to get his emotions under control before he saw Agatha. She was very intuitive, especially where he was concerned, and she'd know something was wrong.

It was the only news that could have elicited this kind of response. His past had come back to haunt him. The only case he'd worked that had ever gone unsolved. The Copper Cove Boys had robbed banks all over the East coast. They were brilliant in their execution, like a military operation. Then they upped the stakes and added murder to their list of crimes.

Hank wasn't proud to say that politics and red tape had gotten in the way of bringing justice to the victims. The FBI wanted to make sure the headlines focused on the robberies and not the murders. It brought better press and looked sexier in print. And the FBI outplayed their hand, setting up a sting that never came to fruition because the Copper Cove Boys got wind of it, took the fortune they'd amassed, and went underground.

"And now they're back," Hank whispered. And the FBI wanted him to help with the investigation.

Even a year or so ago, he would have jumped at the chance to get back on board. His pride was at stake. It was the one case that got away from him, but his priorities had changed. There were other investigators who could lead the charge and bring the ruthless gang down. But not him. He was looking to the future. It was time to get engaged and start his life with Agatha.

He'd been amazed how easily everyone had been able to deceive Agatha into taking the trip to San Antonio for the weekend. Coil's recent suspension and reinstatement as sheriff had played into the scenario perfectly. Agatha hadn't thought a thing of it when Coil said he'd book the trip as a thank you to both of them for stepping up to the plate and taking over while he'd been out, and also for exposing all the corruption that had been going on during the election.

Agatha had been thrilled for the chance to get away, and hadn't asked too many questions.

"This is exciting," she said, looking out the window as their plane landed. "We're both in need of a break and this is going to be perfect. I'm going to eat my way through pounds of chips and salsa."

Hank chuckled. The gleam in her eyes was like that of a kid in a candy store. "And when you get too full, I'll roll you back to the hotel so you can fall into a carb coma."

"That's one of the many reasons I love you," she said, squeezing his hand.

Hank let out a breath when he saw the driver waiting for them at the airport. Everything was going according to plan. He owed Heather big time. Check-in went smoothly, and the concierge gave him a thumbs up out of Agatha's view. Hank hoped that meant the champagne and chocolate covered strawberries were waiting in their room.

Hank had lived life on a policeman's budget, so he'd never stayed in a hotel like this one before. It was built like a fort, complete with stone battlements and cannons in the parapets. The décor was lush and expensive and old, and he saw from the placard on the wall that it had, in fact, been a real fort during the Mexican-American War.

The man who'd checked them in was guiding them to their suite in the top tower. The suite had two bedrooms and two baths, but was connected by a common living area. The temptation had been enormous, but they'd both been careful to keep separate living quarters, at home and when they traveled. He *really* hoped they had a short engagement.

"Wow," Agatha said, when their guide opened the door and let them in. "Gorgeous."

Hank barely noticed the open space or the balcony that looked out over the Riverwalk. The champagne and strawberries were laid out next to a bouquet of flowers, just as planned, but his throat was closing up and he started to feel the panic of what was to come.

"You okay?" she asked, putting a hand on his arm.

"Yeah, I'm just warm," he said, and tipped the hotel employee before shutting the door behind him.

"Is that a hot tub in the corner?" Agatha asked.

Hank chuckled uncomfortably, but it came out more as a croak.

"Everything is beautiful," she said, smelling the bouquet of yellow roses.

"Happy Valentine's Day," he said, his voice hoarse.

The smile that spread across her face was worth every worry and all the hours of time spent planning for the weekend.

"I love it," she said, her eyes glistening with tears.

It was then he realized how little time he spent trying to romance Agatha. He took her no-nonsense attitude and drive to get the job done for granted. She still had these hidden soft spots, and it was important for him to remember that.

She threw herself into his arms and kissed him, surprising him with her enthusiasm. By the time she let go, they were both out of breath.

"Wow," she said again, blushing this time. "This really is special. I'm so glad you attacked me on your lawn the first day we met."

He barked out a laugh in surprise. "You tripped over the sprinkler."

"Yes, after you blasted me with a garden hose."

"You were trespassing."

"There's no such thing in a small town," she said. "I was just being neighborly."

"Nosy," he corrected. "Champagne?"

"Of course," she said.

He poured her a glass and made her a plate with the strawberries. "We have dinner reservations in a couple of hours. I suggest you take these, put some bubbles in the tub, and soak until you're pruny. I'll meet you back out here at eighteen-thirty."

Hank tried to nap, but he was too wired, so he turned on the TV. When that didn't hold his attention he went ahead and showered and dressed in his dark gray suit and a pale purple shirt and tie the woman at the store helped him pick out.

He'd left his champagne untouched, wanting a clear head, and he was pacing back and forth in their common area when he heard her door open. He turned to face her and the spit dried up in his mouth and his lungs stopped working.

She wore a dress the color of crushed strawberries, and it skimmed her long, lean body in a way that made him want to keep her all to himself and not let any other man set eyes on her. The strappy black shoes had her standing slightly taller than him, but he didn't mind. Agatha was simply a natural beauty, with eyes that changed between blue and green, dark lashes, and dark hair she'd been letting grow and let hang in loose curls around her shoulders. Hank loved that she was comfortable with who she was, and her confidence drew every eye to her when she was in a crowd.

"Wow," Hank stumbled over what to say.

Her smile lit the room. "Thanks," she said. "I'm ready when you are."

Their driver took them to the historic district to what looked like a renovated old hacienda turned restaurant. It was simple and elegant, and there were several well-dressed couples being let out at the front doors for the special Valentine's dinner.

Despite the number of couples, the tables weren't crammed in so they were all sitting on top of each other. They were led to a corner table near the fireplace that was secluded and romantic.

"I'm impressed," Agatha said. "You've pulled out all the stops."

Hank just smiled, reminding himself to thank Heather again. He was even able to sit with his back to the wall so he could observe the entire room. Police habits never died.

Wine would be served with each course, and they got lost in conversation like they normally did. But the proposal was all he could think about. When should he do it? After the appetizer? During dessert?

He didn't think he could wait, so he slipped his hand into his coat pocket and grabbed the ring box. He shifted his weight to slide from the chair smoothly onto one knee, and he sucked in a deep breath just before the restaurant erupted in applause.

Across the room was another man who'd just stolen Hank's thunder and proposed to the shocked woman sitting across from him. Hank tightened his fist in frustration and let go of the ring box so it stayed in his pocket. He'd wait until the next course.

He'd felt more relaxed after the appetizer and first wine course, so he cleared his throat and decided to try again. He reached for the box just as the restaurant erupted in applause yet again. He growled aloud this time, causing Agatha to look at him with concern.

It happened again after the salad course. And again after the main course. Dessert was going to be his turn, come hell or high water, and he looked around the restaurant ferociously daring anyone to contradict him.

"Agatha," Hank said, stopping their conversation abruptly.

He grasped the ring box and scooted his chair back so it scraped across the wooden floor. And he moved to get down on one knee just as there was a collective gasp through the restaurant. He scanned the restaurant, looking for his nemesis, and his gaze locked on his target. The man and his new fiancée looked like they'd already had too much to drink.

"Hank, are you all right?" Agatha asked, her attention caught between him and the happy couple.

He was so focused on his plans being interrupted that it barely registered when his enemy shook the champagne bottle before he tried to open it. Hank saw the sommelier rush toward the man, trying to head him off before he drenched everyone around him in champagne. But it was too late.

Hank heard the resounding *pop* of the cork that seemed more like a gunshot in the closed-in space, and then he felt nothing but pain as the cork found its target right in the center of his forehead. He slid from his chair, the world spinning, and then there was nothing but black.

CHAPTER TWO

"Hank? You okay, partner?"

Hank heard the voice, but it sounded muffled, as if he were underwater. It wasn't Agatha's voice. Maybe a waiter or an EMT? But how did they know his name? That champagne cork must've knocked him out cold.

"Hank, you need me to get Doc Sutherland?" the voice asked.

"Doc Sutherland?" Hank answered, his voice hoarse. "Who's that? Just a champagne cork. I'll be fine."

"Champagne cork?" the man asked, confused. "You got kicked in the head by old Bessie. You know she's mean as the devil."

Hank rubbed his forehead, and felt the knot the size of a golf ball. His head was pounding, and his vision blurry.

"Bessie?" Hank asked, confused.

"How many fingers I got up?" asked the man.

It hurt to look at anything, so Hank closed his eyes and focused on breathing. "Who are you?" he asked.

"It's worse than we thought," said a different man. "He don't even know who we are."

Hank tried to open his eyes again, and realized only the right one would open. The left was swollen shut. And why was the sun glaring in his good eye? It was nighttime.

"Hey, Springer. How about you go get the doc? Looks like Hank is the one who got hammered this time."

"You got it," Springer said.

"James?" Hank asked, recognizing the voice.

"Hey, you remember me," James said. "That's good."

"What are you doing here? Where's Aggie?"

Hank felt hands on his shoulders, trying to lift him to a sitting position, and he thought he might be sick to his stomach.

"I work here," James said.

"At the restaurant?" Hank asked, confused.

"Restaurant?" James chuckled. "What's a restaurant? This is the livery stable."

"Stable?" Hank scowled. "Like a barn? With horses?"

"That's right."

"So that's what I smell," Hank said, gagging. "I thought it was the French cheese."

"Only thing French in this town is Marie Cavelier, and I don't think that's cheese she's selling in those upstairs rooms. What you're smellin' is good old-fashioned horse manure. Got your hand right in it."

Hank moved his hand as far away from his nose as he could, determined not to look at the offending limb.

"Where's Aggie?" Hank asked.

James pursed his lips. "You mean Miss Harley?"

Hank nodded.

"She's over at the newspaper office," James said. "Why?"

"I need to call her. Where's my cell?"

"Bessie must have knocked something loose. Why

11

would you have a cell with you? The cells are over at the jail."

"Phone," Hank correcting, his head pounding even more. "Give me my phone so I can call her."

"Hank, I don't know what in the Sam Hill you're talking about," James said. "You're talking crazy. I think you better lay back down until Doc can get here."

Hank had had enough of this prank. Maybe the guys rushed down to San Antonio when they heard he was in the hospital, but it was time to get some facts and fresh air, preferably the latter first.

Hank's vision was blurred, and he'd had enough concussions in his lifetime to know he had a doozy. Flies buzzed around his head, and he swiped at them with his clean hand.

"Someone tell me what's going on," he said, anger making his voice louder than normal. Something he instantly regretted.

"You took a hard blow to the head," James said. "You've been out cold for some time."

"The cork hit me," he insisted.

"Bessie got a good lick in," James said. "You know how ornery she can be. Mean as the devil."

"Is Bessie a cork?" he asked, confused

James stared at him for a few seconds, clearly unsure how to proceed. "Bessie's a horse, ya daft man. You ride one every day."

Hank felt like his brains were scrambled eggs. "You mean I ride a HOG every day," he said, thinking of his motorcycle.

James roared with laughter, sending spikes of pain through Hank's head. "If that don't beat all. You'd be the talk of the town riding through on a pig."

"Not a pig," Hank growled. "A HOG. A Harley Davidson motorcycle. My HOG."

"Boss, you ain't got no hog. Jed Blue is the only pig man in these parts. You're crazy as a loon."

Hank decided it best to change the direction of the conversation. They weren't getting anywhere, and he still didn't have a clue what was going on.

"Where am I?"

"You're on Main Street," James said, speaking slowly. "In the livery stable. You've been here a million times."

How in the world had he gone from proposing marriage to Agatha to laying in horse manure in a time that was clearly meant to look like the old west? Maybe it was all a horrible dream. Or maybe everyone had gotten together to play an elaborate prank on him.

"When did y'all get to San Antonio?" Hank asked.

"When you sent for us," James said.

"And when was that?"

"About two years ago. You sent me a telegram and asked me to come work for you."

"A telegram?" Hank's voice trembled.

"Yep," James beamed with pride.

"Is this a dream?"

"Seems like a nightmare, boss, but who knows, you might enjoy laying in the middle of all this manure. I'd prefer to get up if it's all the same to you."

Hank hesitated, but knew he needed to ask a very important question. "What day is it?"

"February fourteenth."

"And the year?" he asked.

"Eighteen seventy-four."

Hank collapsed back onto the dusty ground, his head swimming and his breath coming in short gasps.

"Hey, Marshal Davidson. You okay?" asked an unfamiliar voice.

Had he passed out? He didn't have time to think before his head was dunked under water. He sputtered and tried to breathe, and he was dunked once more.

"He's comin' around," James said. "Looks mad as a hornet."

Whoever'd had him by the scruff of the neck let go, and Hank went face first into the trough. He came up gasping, his head still throbbing, and hair dripping in his face. He rinsed his hands off while he was down there, and took a moment to gather his thoughts. He finally pushed himself up and scanned the faces around him, familiar, but unfamiliar.

"Welcome back," said the old man. His bi-focal specs rested at the very tip of a slender, red nose, and Hank could only guess this was the Doc. "You all right, son?"

"No, I don't think I am," Hank said. His left eye was finally starting to open, and he looked at his surroundings. His mind couldn't reconcile what his eyes saw, but he was a trained investigator who dealt in fact. The facts, as he could process them, were that nothing made sense.

He was wearing a denim shirt and a brown leather vest, and his pants were also denim, but were cut differently than anything he'd seen before. His boots were dusty, and he wore spurs. He ran his hand over the leather of his vest, and he rested his fingers on the silver star pinned there. He was a marshal.

"When did I become a marshal?" He asked.

The men all looked at each other, but it was Springer who answered. "You was hired as marshal about two years ago. That's when you sent them telegrams for me and James to come and help you straighten out this lawless town."

Hank's mind began to clear, and he tried to stitch together the facts as he knew them. He knew that on Valentine's Day he'd taken a blow to the head from a champagne bottle's cork while proposing to Agatha. He knew he'd woken up in the year 1874 and though the players were the same, things were very different.

He clearly had some type of head trauma, and panicking would only make things worse. The logical thing to do was to play out the scenario until his brain could catch up with reality.

"I'm fine," Hank said. "Just a little addled."

The men nodded and Springer held out a well-crafted leather gun belt that held two pistols and a cartridge belt filled with bullets that crossed over his chest. "You might want this, Boss."

"Right," Hank said, strapping on the belt with shaking hands.

There was a sudden commotion from behind and what sounded like a thundering herd heading in their direction. The ground shook, and dust exploded with every stamp of hooves. Hank stared in wide-eyed surprise. It looked so real.

"Take cover," James yelled.

Wood exploded off the hitching post and several shards struck Hank in the neck and face. The smell of blood and the warmth as it trickled down his cheek and the scruff of his beard shot him into action.

He dropped to the ground and rolled behind the trough for cover, pulling his weapon from the holster as if it were second nature. Bullets were flying everywhere, and self-preservation mode kicked in and he returned fire. The Colt .44 packed a punch.

"Someone get Doc inside," Hank yelled, thinking the old man was a sitting duck.

"Got 'em," Springer yelled.

"I'm taking the high ground," James called out. "I'll cover you."

The bandits stopped at the end of Main Street. Hank didn't see if any of them were thrown from their steeds, but he doubted that they were expecting such an immediate response to their charge.

"Who are they?" Hank asked.

"That's the Copper Cove Boys," Springer whispered.

Hank froze. Even in an alternate reality the Copper Cove Boys haunted him.

"I don't see Dillon McIrish," Hank said, speaking of the gang's leader.

"Ranger Coil is transporting McIrish to the military outpost around Austin for safekeeping until his trial."

Another round of gunfire erupted, but the gang had split up so they could surround their targets. Hank realized that *he* was the target. He was a marshal after all. He heard the sound of a rifle firing overhead as James laid down cover for them to return fire.

Hank ripped two shots back in the direction of where the bullets were coming. He fired more into the sky than at anyone. He wasn't sure where there were innocent bystanders. They were in the middle of town after all.

"James," Hank said.

"Yeah, boss?"

"On the count of three I want you to lay down cover fire to the south and east. We need to get somewhere with better protection. We'll end up trapped here if we stay."

"Okay, but we got bad news," James said.

"Worse than being surrounded by a band of outlaws?" Hank asked.

"Dillon McIrish is leading the pack."

Hank's heart stopped in his chest. "Yeah, that is worse."

CHAPTER THREE

The Sharps Buffalo Rifle ripped a round that screamed straight down Main Street. The echo reverberated off the saloon, the jail, the bank, and the church, but the most damage was done to whatever or whomever the .50 caliber bullet made contact with.

"Enough," Agatha Harley shouted, her pulse pounding in her ears. "Y'all get out of this town right now."

The long-range rifle had been a gift, and she'd found she had a talent for shooting. She reached into her pants pocket for another bullet and slipped the round into the chamber. Her hope was that the warning shot would've been enough to run them off, but in the event they'd come for a real battle, she was ready. Besides, that was her man pinned down behind the water trough.

Her fury got the better of her and she didn't bother taking cover. Agatha almost dared the Copper Cove Boys to take aim at her. Sure, she was the only woman in town crazy enough to wear denims, but there was no mistaking her for one of the boys.

Agatha had moved down to San Antonio a few years

earlier to work for the paper as an investigative reporter. She'd found that as a woman, people wouldn't mind what they said in front of her, thinking her brain was full of fluff, but she had a reputation as determined, like a dog gnawing a bone, and she wouldn't rest until she had the whole story.

And the Copper Cove Boys were news. They'd been terrorizing the area, so businesses and families alike were afraid of what each day might hold. It had been her that had exposed each member of the gang, hoping the news would spread from town to town and someone might take a lucky shot at them. It had painted a target on her back, but she didn't care. The people who moved here deserved to live their lives in peace.

"One day I'm going to have enough of you, Agatha Harley," Dillon McIrish yelled. His words echoed down the deserted street.

What was he doing back in town? Coil was supposed to be escorting him to Austin for trial.

Agatha aimed in the direction of McIrish's voice, and she braced herself as she pulled the trigger. Her vision blurred with the concussion of the primer striking. It created a deafening sound as another monster size projectile hurled down Main Street and in the direction where she assumed McIrish would be.

Agatha watched with satisfaction as dust plumed into the air and their horses took off out of town. She dropped to one knee and quickly worked to prep the weapon for another round if needed. She'd run into these bad guys before and didn't trust any of them. It wouldn't have been a surprise had they tried to circle back behind her.

She waited several minutes before she shouldered the rifle and sprinted toward the livery.

"Hank," Agatha called out. "Hank, you okay?"

She noticed James climbing down from atop the barn. He had an intense grin as he started heading their way too. Agatha's heart pounded once she neared their hiding place and didn't see anyone moving.

"Hank?"

"Over here, Aggie," Hank said. "We had to get Doc out of the line of fire."

She and James hurried into the stable. Hank and Springer had Doc Sutherland propped up on a few bails of hay.

"Doc," she said, worry in her voice. "What happened?"

Hank caught her in a hug, and she noticed the goose egg on his forehead, but he seemed to be fine.

"What happened to Doc?" she asked. "Was he shot?"

"I'm okay," Doc said, gasping for air. "These boys carried me when I fell trying to escape the gunfight. I'm too old for this stuff." He winked at her. "Don't worry about me. It's Ranger Coil we should be worried about."

"You're right," James said. "Coil would never let a man escape unless he was unable to stop him."

That was a sobering thought and she shook her head. "No," she said. "I won't believe Coil is dead. We need to find him."

Hank's face looked grim.

"We need to get Doc home," James said. "Before his wife hears what happened. She'll be worried sick. Springer and I will take him."

"Good idea," Hank said. He reached down and grabbed his Stetson off the dusty floor and slapped it against his thigh. Then he walked right out of the back of the livery, leaving Agatha behind.

"Oh, no you don't," she said, running after him. She called his name, and he stopped but didn't turn back to face her. He stared out at the wide open space, his hand resting comfortably on his pistol.

"What's wrong, baby?"

"You gotta stop calling me that in public," he said.

She just grinned. "You and I both know you love it. Tell me what's going on."

"If Coil is dead, it's my fault," Hank said. "I had a chance to put McIrish behind bars before I left Philadelphia to come south. He'd killed two people in a bank robbery, but politics changed my investigation and he got away."

"That isn't your fault," she assured him. "That's on those folks back east. And if we're using your logic, then I'm responsible too. I'm the one who started writing those newspaper articles about him terrorizing the county. It's thanks to the circulation that things have escalated."

"I guess we got a duty to Coil," Hank said, reaching for her hand and pulled her close. "We either have to rescue him or avenge him."

Agatha looked deep into Hank's hard brown eyes. The man had seen so much in his career as a top-notch lawman. She saw determination and loyalty that would stop at nothing to save him. It was all of those things that had attracted her to Hank when he first arrived in town. But it was the tenderness of his heart that led her to love him.

"I'm with you, no matter what," Agatha said. "I should've aimed higher with old Annie," she said, patting her rifle.

Her newspaper business had done well since the Copper Cove Boys' reign of terror. People were as fascinated by them as they were terrified. Some accused her of profiteering off their crimes, but she and Hank both knew that was a load of bull. The only chance of drawing attention to the gang in the isolated west was to get the attention of fat cat lawmakers in the east. In a way, Agatha knew that it was her paper that had turned the law onto them, but she'd also immortalized them as infamous bandits in a lawless Wild West.

"Aggie, that rifle is going to get you into a mess of trouble," Hank said.

She shrugged. "I don't care. Those boys tried burning down my print shop after McIrish was arrested by the Texas Rangers. I shot the torch right out of one of the bandit's hands before he could set it ablaze."

Hank rolled his eyes. "I know, Aggie. I was right there with you."

"Oh, yeah," she said, grinning. "You did good too."

Hank squeezed her hand. "Can I ask you something? It might sound crazy."

"Sure, baby."

"Are we engaged to be married?"

"You must've taken a lick to that rock-hard head of yours," she said. "No, we aren't engaged."

"Oh, okay," he said, looking confused and embarrassed.

She decided she might as well tell him the truth. "Honestly, I've got no idea what you've been waiting for."

Maybe she should ask him to marry her. Folks in San Antonio thought she was half crazy anyway. She wore trousers, lived alone, and mostly did what, and went where, she wanted. Her independence was fierce, but it had never bothered Hank.

"Actually," he said. "I really thought we'd gotten engaged, but I guess Bessie did more damage when she kicked me in the head than I thought."

"So that's what happened?" she asked, looking at the knot.

"Yeah, among other things."

"Since we're on the topic of marriage," she said, steamrolling ahead. "Whaddaya say we do this?"

"Are you proposing to me?" Hank asked, his face going pale.

"Yes," she blurted out. "Yes I am."

"Well, that's a sure surprise," he said. He was just opening his mouth to answer when they were interrupted.

"Marshal," yelled Deputy James. "Marshal, come quick. It's Ranger Coil."

Agatha spun around to see James approaching full speed on his palomino horse. Her knees weakened in fear, as he jerked the reins to a hard stop.

"What's the news on Coil?" Hank pressed.

"His horse turned up at his ranch," James explained. "His wife knew something was wrong, so she rode into town on it to get help."

"Shelly's at the jail?" Agatha asked. "Is anyone with her?"

"Yes, ma'am. We were halfway to getting Doc home when we intercepted her, so we all came back to town."

"Is she alright?" Hank asked.

"It don't look good, boss. I'm not sure if Shelly noticed or not, but the side of Coil's horse saddle is covered in blood. It looks fresh."

"If it's still fresh," she said, "Then maybe it means he was recently wounded, so there's a chance of finding him alive."

"Good point," Hank said with a nod. "Let's head over to the jail and have a closer look."

"Marshal, I'd be glad to give y'all my Bessie to ride back, and I'll walk to the jail," James offered.

Hank stumbled back a step. "I've had enough contact

23

with old Bessie for the moment." He rubbed the baseball-sized lump on his forehead and his eyes began to water again at the memory of that old horse kicking him in the head.

"Fair enough," James said. "But maybe Miss Agatha wants to ride."

"I wish I had my Jeep to take me back to the jail," Agatha said, thinking of the long trip.

"What did you say?" Hank asked

"You know," she said, confused. "Jeep. My horse." Hank must've really been addled to not remember Jeep.

"Right," he said.

Agatha thanked James but waved him on, deciding it was better to hitch up a wagon. It was then she remembered Hank hadn't answered her about the marriage proposal.

CHAPTER FOUR

Hank stashed his rifle before jumping out of the wagon to wrap the leather strap from the horse's reigns around the hitching post. He offered a hand to Agatha, but she waved him off and hopped over the side.

"I got it," she said.

Lordy, she was a handful. It didn't seem to matter in which time he lived.

The old county jail was a one-story structure made of solid timber. The interior had wood floors, and two cells faced with steel bars that were simple but effective. Sun streamed in a side window, and although there was a red curtain hung over it, the draft from the rafters kept it from blocking the light.

Hank saw Shelly, Coil's wife, as soon as they walked inside. She jumped up from behind the desk, her face tear-streaked and lined with worry.

"Shelly," he said, not really knowing what to say. "I'm so sorry." He felt the crushing weight of those words. They seemed inadequate. He didn't even think it had really sunk in yet. The reality was Coil was most likely dead. They all knew it, but no one wanted to say it.

"What happened?" she asked.

"It's McIrish and the Copper Cove Boys," Springer said.

If anything, Shelly went paler and she collapsed in the chair behind the desk.

Hank glared at Springer. The boy never could keep his mouth shut.

"Why don't James and Springer take me around back so I can check out Coil's horse," Agatha said, trying to diffuse the tension and give Hank some privacy with Shelly.

"Good idea," Hank said. "I'll meet y'all around back." He waited until Agatha and the deputies had cleared the room before asking, "Have you heard anything else about the trip Coil was taking to Austin?"

Shelly shook her head. "He told me before he left he couldn't tell me where or why he was going. He said there were too many eyes and ears along the way, and it was safer for me not to know."

"Reggie was escorting a prisoner to a military camp," he said and hesitated a bit. "It was Dillon McIrish, and from the looks of things, McIrish escaped his hold."

"You think he's dead, don't you?" she asked, eyes dry and devastated.

"I think we're going to find him, no matter what, and bring him home to you."

"Thank you," she said, nodding. "That means a lot to me. And it'd mean a lot to Reggie too."

The front door swung open and Hank immediately put his hand on his weapon as a silhouette filled the doorway.

"Whoa, Marshal," a voice said. "It's me, Karl Johnson."

"Karl?" Hank asked.

"I heard there was trouble, so I left the ranch to offer my aid. I didn't know you were going to shoot me over it."

"I appreciate the help," he said. "Would you mind taking Shelly home and keeping an eye out around their place for the time being? If Coil is alive, then McIrish might try and make a play for his family as revenge."

"You can count on me, Marshal," Karl said.

Hank said his goodbyes and then went out back to join Agatha and his deputies. "How's it looking?" he asked.

"The blood is mostly on the left side of the saddle and horse, so I think that's the direction Coil must have slid off."

"Slid?" Hank asked. "He didn't fall?"

"I think so," she said. "The blood is swiped from the horn of the saddle and smeared going down. Also, it looks like Coil's spurs dug into the horse's right side and scraped across his hide."

"What does that mean?" Hank asked.

"It means it's possible he's still alive somewhere," Agatha said. "Coil is resourceful. He'd know how to hide. I have to believe he's still alive. I can't imagine the alternative."

Hank agreed. Coil was his best friend. They'd been through too much together for things to end like this.

"Now what?" Springer asked.

There was no time for answers because gunfire erupted. Everyone ducked for cover, and Hank pulled Agatha beneath him as he knelt into a shooting position. He felt her pushing against him

"I can take care of myself, Hank Davidson," she yelled.

"Yeah, with what?"

"My rifle," she said, then must've realized she'd left it on the wagon. "Crud."

"You're welcome," he said, rubbing it in.

27

James motioned for them to come where he was behind the cover of the jail. "It looks like a bank robbery," he said once they'd gotten closer.

"How you figure?" Springer asked.

"I saw two of the Copper Cove Boys riding in circles shooting in the air, but then I saw a whole bunch of them hang a right without shooting. It looks like they were trying to ride under the chaos caused by the other two."

"A diversion," Agatha said with a gasp.

"We gotta act now," Hank said.

"There was a bunch of them, boss," James said, nervously. "There's only the three of us."

"Four," Agatha said, narrowing her eyes.

"Three," Springer said.

"I got more experience shooting at those thugs than any of you," she said, and spun off toward the wagon. Hank assumed she was going to retrieve her rifle. He knew there'd be no stopping her and to be quite honest, they needed the help.

"How we gonna handle this, Marshal?" James asked.

Hank's pulse quickened. His mind raced. He knew the Copper Cove Boys like the back of his hand. And if they were the same in the Old West as they were in the future, then he knew exactly what they'd do.

Agatha came back with her rifle and he nodded. "I know how they're going to pull this off. I've seen it before."

"Back east?" James asked.

"That's right," Hank said, not going into detail. "It's all about smoke and mirrors."

"Huh?" James asked.

"Distractions," Hank said quickly. "They'll all go into the bank, and all but one will come back out, making a ruckus and drawing attention to themselves. But there will be one of them slipping out the back. He's the one carrying the loot. Then they'll meet up at a specific location and divvy it up." Then he explained the plan.

"We better get moving," Agatha said.

He'd noticed the horses in a little paddock to the side of the jail, but he hadn't realized they were *his* horses. Or at least police horses. But everyone mounted up while he stood there looking at the black beast that pawed at the ground restlessly when he got close.

"What's my horse's name?" Hank asked.

"Beemer," Springer said. "Your head still smarting you, Marshal?"

"I guess so," Hank said and swung up into the saddle.

The team moved down a back street and through an alley to get in the proper positions, and Hank gave instructions along the way. He'd decided to go with the ultimate fake out to make the Copper Cover Boys think they had been fooled. He and Springer would confront the big group of gangsters as they exited the front door. Agatha and James would go around back to intercept the real crook and recover the bank's cash. It was a gamble, but he had equal confidence in both of their abilities.

Hank and Springer took position behind the hardware store right across the street from the bank's front entrance. There was a line of eight horses stretched across the center hitching post.

Everyone had cleared the street at the first sign of trouble, and doors and windows had been bolted. But he could feel the eyes of everyone watching.

If Hank were wrong about the decoy, he and James would be fatally outnumbered and outgunned. He also began to reconsider the wisdom of placing only two at the back. The gang's ruse in the future was to sneak one man out, but that didn't mean they'd used the same ploy in 1874. What if James and Agatha were equally matched? Or worse?

Hank held onto Beemer's reins as the horse began to grow restless. There were shouts from inside, but thankfully, no gunfire. It seemed an eternity passed before the double wooden doors of the bank swung open, and the Copper Cove Boys swarmed through the doors like ants. The eight men all wore dark overcoats and black hats, and they had bandanas stretched over their faces. They hooted and hollered, and then they raised their guns and shot off rounds into the sky. Hank guessed they didn't know or didn't care that what went up must eventually come down.

"That's not a good sign," Hank whispered.

"What's that?" Springer asked, worry in his eyes.

It was now or never. Hank trusted his experience and instinct, but this scene was more like a bad spaghetti western than a real life crime in progress.

"I said, that's our sign," Hank lied. "Go in under control and take charge immediately. Unless we act as if we think they'd just robbed the place, they'll know it's a trap."

"But they did just rob the bank. They might not be holding the loot, but they robbed it all the same."

"Good point. Let's go," Hank said.

The outnumbered pair charged toward Camellia Street before cutting a hard right back into the hive of violent marauders.

"This is the law," Hank yelled. "Everybody freeze!"

Laughter, curses and taunts greeted them. Hank had one eye on the bandits and the other on his deputy. He needed Springer to have his head in the game and remain cool.

Hank flinched as two blasts fired close to him, and he

30

thought they were both goners. But it was Springer's six-shooter that had been fired.

"Put your hands in the air, or we'll start filling ya up with led!" Springer ordered.

The bandits laughed. "This is our town now. We're the law."

"Wanna bet?" Springer holstered his revolver and slipped the wooden-stocked rifle from the smooth leather pouch attached to the right side of his English riding saddle.

Hank tried not to let his surprise show on his face. When had Springer turned into Dirty Harry?

"You'll be the first one I drop," Springer said with a snarl.

The man narrowed evil eyes at Springer, but he slowly eased his hands up.

"You feeling lucky, punk?" Hank asked, pointing his own rifle at a swarthy looking man who was trying to sneak around the side of the bank.

"Y'all are under arrest for bank robbery," Springer declared.

Hank's glare narrowed beneath a furrowed brow. His focus was intense as they laughed again.

"We didn't rob no bank," Evil Eyes called out. "How about y'all walk away nice and quiet before someone gets hurt?"

"If you didn't rob the bank then you shouldn't mind proving it to us," Hank said. "If you're innocent then everyone can just go on about their business. Y'all drop your weapons and turn out your coat pockets and satchels."

"There's only two of you," Evil Eyes said, his teeth gleaming black as he smiled.

Then Hank heard the cock of another rifle, and he glanced up at the hotel across the street to see a rifle pointed out one of the windows. And then another cock of a gun from somewhere else, and he realized the citizens were helping out.

"I don't think so," Hank said.

The Copper Cove Boys shared a look and then dropped their weapons, opening their trench coats and emptying their pockets. They were clear. And that's when he saw Agatha from the corner of his eye giving him the signal.

"See, boys," Hank called out. "That wasn't hard. Why don't y'all head on out of town?"

Hank waited until they mounted up and left before he nudged Beemer in the opposite direction and back toward the jail. They wouldn't have too long to wait before the gang realized their partner with the loot wasn't going to show up, and they'd eventually retrace their steps back to town.

"Did they get him?" Springer asked.

"We're about to find out."

CHAPTER FIVE

Agatha was out of breath with exhilaration. They'd actually pulled it off. Not only did they recover the bank's money, but they managed to capture one of McIrish's top henchmen.

"We did it!" she said as soon as Hank and Springer walked inside the jail. She knew she sounded like a child, but she couldn't contain her excitement, and that was saying something coming from a woman who liked to live her life on the edge.

Hank grinned. "I knew you could do it."

"It was all you, Boss," James replied. "That was a brilliant plan. How'd you know?"

"Experience."

"You should've seen James," Agatha said. "He gave that robber one chance to surrender. That creep went for his pistol, and then *wham*! He knocked him out cold."

Agatha imitated the way James had uppercut the crook, her leather hat flipping off her head.

"Which one did we get?" Springer asked.

"Cornbread Dodger," James said. "I recognized him from the feature Agatha did in the paper."

"Cornbread?" Springer asked. "Why they call him Cornbread?"

"Because his first name is Roger," Hank said. "Would you want to be called Roger Dodger?"

"Good point," Springer said.

"How do you know so much about him?" Agatha asked. "I didn't know his first name."

"Experience," Hank said again. "I've been dealing with these outlaws for a long time. There's not much I don't know about them."

"Well, maybe Roger Dodger will know you too," Agatha said. "We need him to spill the beans about Coil."

"I ain't saying nothing," Cornbread groaned from the cell, holding his aching jaw.

"I'd suggest you wait to speak until you're spoken to," Agatha said, and then she added insult to injury and said, "Roger Dodger. That's a ridiculous name."

The short, stocky bull of a man leapt to his feet and rattled the cage. "Let me out of here! You're all dead! You know that? They'll come for you now!" He reached for a weapon, but his holsters were empty.

"Looks like you're unarmed and all alone, Roger," Agatha said, taunting him.

"Oh, yeah?" Cornbread said, brandishing a knife from the inside of his tattered duster. "Come and get it."

The distinctive cock of a gun echoed in the small room, and Agatha aimed her sidearm directly at Cornbread's head.

"You think we're playing games with you?" Agatha asked. "Do you really?"

Cornbread dropped the knife onto the floor, and James kicked it across the room.

"Got anything else you want to show off?" she asked, then nodded in satisfaction as he took a step back away from the bars.

"How about we advise him of his Miranda Rights before we start questioning him," Hank suggested.

"What?" James asked.

Agatha looked suspiciously at Hank. What had he said about that scumbag in the cell having rights? And who was Miranda? His head injury was obviously still affecting him.

Hank's expression tightened and he rubbed at the knot on his head. "Nevermind."

"Okay, Cornbread," James said. "Let's get down to business. We don't want you. We want to know what happened to Ranger Coil."

Cornbread flashed a row of brown teeth, and Agatha flinched as he let loose a maniacal laugh that made her flesh crawl.

"You ain't getting nothing out of me," Cornbread said. "My boys will be here in no time."

"Your boys?" Agatha asked.

"The Copper Cove Boys," he announced. "They're going to overrun this dump like a swarm of ants on a picnic."

"You think that your criminal band of brothers will raid a town jail to break you free after having robbed a bank?" she asked, chuckling. "You really are an idiot."

His hands strangled the metal bars, and if looks could kill...

"Let's play this out, and see if you can catch on," she said. "You go in with eight other bandits to rob a bank. They

35

all get confronted by the law, but they don't have the money, so they go free."

"Sounds about right," he said, scratching his wooly beard.

"But the one guy the gang let slip out back with all of the stolen cash has mysteriously vanished. They don't know where you are," she said. "For all you know, they think you've high-tailed it out of town with their money."

"They saw you take me in," he said, but he'd gone a little pale.

"Who saw?" she asked. "We took you around back, and then you got your lights knocked out."

"He sucker punched me," Cornbread said.

"No, he hit you fair and square. You just gotta nice, soft jaw. Too bad your skull is so thick," she said. "If you were a thinking kind of man, you'd have figured out by now that your gang is out hunting for you. I'd even go so far as to bet that when you show up empty-handed they'll put a bullet or two into you before you can start explaining. They don't seem like the trusting kind."

"They'll believe me," he said, but he didn't seem convinced.

"Really?" she asked, leaning back against Hank's wooden desk. "You've got no proof that you were here. Heck, we sure ain't going to confirm it. And there you go running back to your boys without their share of the cash. Do you really think they're going to buy that story about you being arrested and then miraculously set free?"

"Yeah," he said.

"Then why aren't you in jail?" she asked.

"I am in jail," he said, confusion marring his ugly face. "See?"

Agatha pushed herself off the desk, and sauntered over

to the far wall. There was a hook with a single key on a large ring. She slipped one finger in the loop and lifted the key before walking to the cell and unlocking it.

"Not anymore," she said. "You look like a free man to me." The iron bars creaked as she opened them wide.

Cornbread backed away from the open door as if it were a bear trap. "If I walk out that door y'all will fill me full of lead for trying to escape."

"We won't shoot you," Agatha said. "But Dillon McIrish will."

"He trusts me," Cornbread said again.

"Okay," she said. "Bye-bye then."

Cornbread took three steps and stood square in the open threshold. "I'm gonna leave, and they're gonna trust me," he said, not sounding as convinced as he had before.

"See ya," Agatha said, and moved over to the piles of cash they'd spread out on the desk, thumbing through a stack.

Cornbread's eyes never left the money, and he licked his lips once before stepping back inside the cell and closing the door behind him.

"How you gonna keep me alive?" he asked.

"We find Coil, and then we'll talk about you," she said. "He'd better be alive, or else."

"That wasn't part of the deal, lady."

"You telling me he's dead?" she asked, raising a brow.

Agatha held her breath. She didn't want to look away or at the others. She could only imagine what was going through their minds, and she couldn't afford to show Cornbread any weakness or emotion.

"I'm just saying that wasn't part of the deal," he said. "I don't know if he's dead or alive. All I know is that McIrish shot him, and that Ranger fell off his horse just before clearing the tree line toward Golden Eagle Pass."

"Why'd McIrish shoot him?" Hank asked, interrupting.

Agatha stepped back. She was growing fatigued with the high level of stress involved in the cat and mouse game of mental manipulation. She also knew that it was important for a sworn law enforcement officer to take information regarding the possibility of a murder committed by Dillon McIrish.

"We watched them as they headed toward Austin," Cornbread said. "We waited until they got into no-man's land before we ambushed them, and once they rode into Golden Eagle, old Cactus gave the signal. He's second in command."

"Signal to what?" Hank pressed.

Cornbread leaned against the metal bars. He nodded for some water. It had turned stuffy inside the jail with everyone huddled around and only a slight breeze wafting through an open window. Hank motioned for Springer to fetch the tin cup and fill it with water.

"Thanks, Sheriff," Cornbread nodded.

"Marshal," Hank clarified. "Now what was it that Cactus signaled?"

"That Ranger never really had a chance. We'd had him surrounded for two days. We moved in like we was told to do, and I grabbed Dillon and cut him loose from the Ranger's saddle grip. Easy as pie."

"Then what?"

Cornbread chugged the last of the warm water. He stretched his thick arm through the narrow openings and shook the cup for more. He flapped his vest to fan himself as he shaded his eyes from the sunlight's glare.

"The Ranger put up a good fight, and broke through the

circle as the horses started rearing up. I thought he was actually going to make it to the tree line, but McIrish grabbed the rifle from my saddle bag and got a bead on him."

"Did you see him go down?" Hank asked.

"He fell to the right," Cornbread said. "McIrish never misses. The horse dragged him a ways and we lost sight of 'em. We didn't bother recovering the body."

"Golden Eagle is a huge area," Hank said, motioning for Springer to hand Cornbread the refill. "Where exactly did y'all set up the ambush?"

The bandit poured the tin cup of water over the top of his bushy head. His hair still stood up on its ends as trickles of moisture snaked across his face.

"The last I saw your friend was just around—"

The crack of a rifle sounded and a single bullet ripped through the open window and struck Cornbread in the hollow of the throat. There wasn't much meat or blood there, so all it did was make a pinprick sized hole going in, but a much larger exit wound.

Cornbread gasped and clasped both hands around his neck, and then dropped dead inside the dingy cell.

Springer drew his pistol as he crouched by the window.

"No need, son," Hank said, getting a clear view of the trail of dust as the horses sped away. "They're long gone."

"We gotta get out to Golden Eagle," Agatha said.

"Yeah," Hank said, nodding. "And before they hunt us down. They're going to be right angry they're not getting their hands on this money."

CHAPTER SIX

Hank formed a search posse and they made plans to ride out toward Golden Eagle Pass before sunrise. He was aware they'd be tracked by the Copper Cove Boys, but if there was even the slightest hope of Coil being alive, they had to make a go of it. The other option was to stay in town and become stationary targets to be picked off by McIrish.

As soon as Cornbread had been killed, Hank sent a telegram to the Texas Rangers for help. If he pulled his crew out to search for Coil, McIrish would ransack the town within a day. No, Hank was well aware of how McIrish operated. He was a terrorist, and whether he was operating in the current age or in the future, McIrish was vicious.

Reliable as ever, Texas Rangers, Will Ellis and Jason Whitehorse, arrived to accompany James, Springer, Karl, Agatha, and Hank out to Golden Eagle Pass. Ellis also arranged for five soldiers from the state militia to hold down the fort in San Antonio until they returned. James and Karl had split off from the group, circling back to see if they were being tracked.

"Y'all doing okay back there?" Hank asked Agatha and Springer.

They'd loaded the wagon with food, ammo, and medical supplies, and Agatha and Springer were guiding the horses. When they found Coil, they knew he'd either need medical treatment or a hearse.

"We're trying our best to keep up," Agatha called back, the aggravation in her voice clear.

Hank laughed. He knew how stubborn she was. She'd wanted to ride, but she'd drive that buggy as long as it meant proving she could keep up, and often outdo, most men.

"So, when you two gonna get hitched?" Will asked in a whisper.

Hank jerked the reins out of reflex and his horse jerked his head in response. Then he glanced back over his shoulder, but Agatha was far enough back that she'd never overhear their conversation.

"Why do you ask?"

"It's kind of obvious." Will said, chuckling. "I can't believe she hasn't proposed to you. She doesn't seem like the patient sort."

Hank felt the heat rise in his cheeks. She had proposed. He'd totally forgotten. And he hadn't given her an answer.

Will laughed again. "She did, didn't she? I knew it."

"Shh," Hank said. "She'll hear you. How'd you know?"

"You ain't the only one trained to read people. You're guilty as charged," Will said. "Why don't you just go ahead and say yes?"

Hank fumbled around his saddle for his canteen, and guzzled a swig of water. His mouth was dry as dust.

"It ain't right for her to ask me," he said. "I want to be the one to ask her."

"Then why haven't you?"

"Not sure," Hank said. "I love her, but I worry about bad things like this situation and bad people like Dillon McIrish, and what that could do to a marriage."

"Hank, I know you still blame yourself for your wife's murder, but there was no way you could've known what would happen. It's not your fault."

Hank had no idea how Will had known about Tammy, but he felt himself stiffen at the mention of her name. He'd spent years trying to let go of the past, and he thought he'd succeeded, but every now and then it snuck up on him.

"I don't want to talk about it," he said. Hank nudged Beemer's flank with his heel and the horse trotted up ahead of Will, moving through the convoy until he caught up to Whitehorse. He wasn't the talkative type like Will. Whitehorse was all business.

"How's it going?" Jason asked.

"Not you too?" Hank asked with a sigh.

"Huh?" Jason asked, shaking his head. "What did I do?"

"Sorry. I need to go back and apologize to Will."

"You seem rattled," Whitehorse said. "I've never seen you like this. Are you okay? Besides that goose egg on your forehead, I mean."

"I'm fine," Hank said. "Will brought up Tammy, and I didn't handle it well."

"Who's Tammy?" he asked.

"Tammy was my wife. She was killed while trying to catch a very bad guy."

"Why was she trying to catch a bad guy?" Jason asked. "You're the marshal."

Hank forgot there were no women in law enforcement yet. "She just got caught up in the wrong place at the wrong time. Will was reassuring me that it wasn't my fault, but honestly, I still blame myself."

"Did you kill her?" Whitehorse asked.

"Of course not!" Hank said, appalled.

"Did you know she was going to be killed?" Jason asked.

"I knew it was a possibility. It always is."

"Are you God?"

"What?" Hank asked, staring at him. "That's crazy."

"Then how could you have known?" Jason asked. "Stop playing God and pretending that you have the power over life and death."

"I'm not playing God," he said. "I just feel guilty."

"Guilt is a choice," Whitehorse said. "You can choose to feel guilty or you can forgive yourself and move forward with Tammy's memories that honor her life and her legacy. It's your choice."

"Easy?" Hank questioned.

"That's a choice too, Hank."

"So I'm just supposed to forget about Tammy and move on?"

"You can never forget, and no one should expect you to. She's a part of who you are. Tammy is not a thing of the past, but a living memory that you get to honor as you choose. But you *can* move on. If you marry Agatha, then the man Agatha gets to know will have been influenced by the woman you were once married to," Whitehorse explained. "Does that make any sense?"

Hank swallowed hard. The saddle rocked and shifted beneath him, but he wasn't feeling the physical affects as much as he felt the immediate need to apologize to Will and take care of long overdue business with Agatha.

"Yeah," he said. "It does."

"When you marry Agatha you can take what you learned from your first marriage, but Agatha isn't Tammy and she never will be. Make sure you're marrying Agatha for her, and not because you're still in love with the past."

Hank nodded and pulled the reins so he circled back to where Will was riding.

"You back?" Will asked.

"I'm sorry," Hank said. "It's a sore spot."

"I understand, old friend, but out here you can't allow emotion to rule you. We're being tracked by outlaws, and when they decide to ambush us, we need to know that everyone has their head on straight."

Hank felt the bitter sting of being chided by a peer. But he deserved it. After all, Will's concern was keeping everyone alive. Including himself. Hank wouldn't have allowed any distractions on high-risk operations, yet here he was the most distracted of the group.

"Sorry," he said again. "And, you are right. It's time to ask her."

"Ask her what?" Agatha called out from behind him.

Hank jumped in his saddle. He looked over his shoulder and there was Agatha and Springer trotting along at an even clip with the horses. Hank hadn't noticed they'd come out of the rocky terrain and onto a flat stretch. And open area meant they were sitting ducks waiting for an ambush.

He heard the rumble of horse's hoofs coming from behind them. If the bandits had decided to launch their attack at that point, it was a grave mistake without the element of surprise.

Will gave the order to take fighting positions. Hank watched as Agatha and Springer rolled off the right side of the wagon to place the structure in between them and whoever was charging.

"Hold the line until they make that corner," Will ordered. "If it's hostile, open fire at will."

Hank had joined Will and Jason as they flanked each side of the wagon. It would be everyone's best chance of protection. Hank glanced at Agatha as he leveled his rifle at whomever was charging up from behind, but she had her rifle up and ready. Lord, she was a sight to behold. He'd never met anyone like her, and he was crazy for not getting her to the altar as soon as he could.

Suddenly, two riders breached the trees and came into the open. They rode fast and hard, and Hank sucked in a breath and steadied his finger on the trigger. As they drew closer, he realized. It was Karl and James.

"Hold fire," he said. "It's Karl and James."

They'd been riding separately from the group to keep an eye on the Copper Cove Boys. The plan was to surround them if they made a play for the wagon, but whatever it was that had caused them to break ranks must've been serious. They were panting as hard as their horses.

"What's going on?" Hank asked, looking to see if there were other riders behind them. "Y'all okay?"

"Marshal, it's the outlaws," Karl said, speaking in broken syllables while catching his breath. "Stage coach." He pointed behind them.

"They were tracking y'all," James said, "But when they saw the stagecoach passing through, they changed their course and followed."

"Whitehorse and I will go after that stagecoach," Will said. "Y'all keep going after Coil."

"No way can I let you go out there outnumbered," Hank said. "Springer and I will ride with y'all. Aggie can stay here with James and Karl. They look like they could use a break."

"We're fine," Karl said.

"Maybe, but your horses need a rest."

45

"Hey," Agatha said. "I'm not staying here with the wagon doing nothing. I'm going with you."

Will cleared his throat. "We can't high tail it after a robbery with a wagon in tow. We'll be lucky to catch up with them before the driver makes it to the switch pass."

"Then I'll unhitch Jeep and ride with y'all," she said.

"You'll do no such thing," Will said. "You will continue moving along toward Golden Eagle Pass. Coil needs you more than a stagecoach driver does."

Agatha's face turned red, and she blew out a breath before turning on her heel and walking away.

Hank followed behind her. "Aggie, I understand how you feel, but Coil is out there, and his life might be measured in minutes. We can't chance his rescue to go chasing after a few bandits looking for cash."

"You're right," she conceded. "You're both right. I'm just so angry that those criminals are trying to ruin our lives that I want to take it out on them.'

"You'll get your chance, but Coil comes first."

"I'll find him," she said.

"I know you will," Hank said.

"Times a wastin', Hank," Will shouted as he and White-horse moved out toward the switch pass.

Hank kissed Agatha on the cheek, and gave her a last look before getting on Beemer and riding off to meet the others.

Whitehorse was skilled at tracking and lead the party. Once they moved away from the flat, smooth meadows of the plains and into a more forested area, the trail was harder to follow. Hank kept watch for anyone who might be waiting to ambush them.

"Heads up," Jason whispered, holding up his hand signaling them to stop. "Something's up ahead."

Hank tried to peer around the three men and their horses, but the thicket and shadows from the dense over-hangs made it tough. It was hard to estimate, but Hank figured they'd been on the go for at least an hour since leaving the rest of them with the wagon.

Hank was able to make out an elevated ridge to the right, and there were open areas straight and to the left. Will motioned for Jason and Springer to dismount and take a high position on the ridge. That would allow them to check for any of the Copper Cove Boys hiding up top, and also allow them a crow's nest vantage point.

The two experienced lawmen tied their reins to a sturdy tree, and began to silently traverse the jagged terrain. Hank was amazed at their stealth and knew he would've come tumbling down in a rock avalanche. Once they were up top, Will signaled for Hank to follow him in a rush around the cliff's edge to ensure an element of surprise.

If there were four or five gun slingers, the two of them would need to move fast and aggressive to secure them.

"You ready?" Will whispered over his shoulder.

Hank felt his chest heave with anticipation and nodded. It was go time. Hank controlled Beemer easily as he secured his revolver in one hand and the reins in the other. They moved swiftly, and Hank immediately saw the stagecoach when they turned past the rocks. It was still a good ways away, but they were closing the gap fast.

They were less than ten yards from the broadside of the stagecoach before Will cut sharp to the right, and Hank reacted by going in the opposite direction. There was no one in sight.

"This is the law," Will shouted. "Anyone out there?"

Four horses were still hitched to the stagecoach, but all was silent.

"You think they killed the driver?" Hank asked.

"I'm the driver," someone called out from behind a bush. "What y'all want?"

"I'm Will Ellis, Texas Ranger. We saw you being chased by the Copper Cove Boys. You okay?"

Hank's heart was pounding. This was either an ambush or a set up. He caught movement in his peripheral vision. It was Whitehorse and Springer scooting down the rocks.

"I saw them boys, but they ain't paid me no mind," the stagecoach driver said. "As soon as they caught up to me, they waved and circled back from where they came."

"They're going for Agatha," Hank said, fear gnawing his gut.

CHAPTER SEVEN

Agatha paced while Karl and James dismounted and caught their breaths. Karl's horse seemed especially winded. "I think we need to get some space in between where we are and where those outlaws last saw us," she suggested.

"Karl can't ride on a lagging horse," James said. "And we need to work as a team. There's too much at stake."

"I understand that," she said patiently. "But he can walk Bacon down to that creek in the woods while we get going. He can catch up later."

"I don't think it's a good idea to split up," Karl said.

James was thoughtful for several minutes before he spoke again. "Agatha is right," he said. "The Copper Cove Boys know our location, and if they decide to come back, we won't have a chance."

"Fine," Karl said. "If that's how you both feel then I'll do it. I won't be long behind you. But be careful and keep your guard up."

"Always," James said.

Agatha was quick to check the hitching on the wagon, and she followed behind James as he took the lead on horseback. She glanced over her shoulder one last time to see Karl leading Bacon into the wooded area.

"I sure hope those outlaws don't find him," she said. "They won't deal kindly with him."

"They won't deal kindly with any of us. I can't believe they killed Cornbread," James said. "Their own man. Vicious."

"We'll keep our eyes and ears open," she said. "How far ahead do you think Coil might be?"

"Hard to say. Cornbread was killed before he had a chance to tell us anything useful. He could be anywhere over the next hundred miles."

"Whatever it takes to find him and bring him home," she said. "I know he'd do the same for one of us."

Agatha wasn't sure what to look for, and she figured calling out Coil's name wouldn't be safe. The truth was, she was out of her element. She could ride and shoot and do all the things men did, but she had no experience when it came to this kind of work. It was exciting and terrifying all at the same time. She didn't know how they lived with those extremes.

"You know," she said, "Worst case scenario, we'd reach the military outpost near Austin and have to turn back and retrace our steps."

"How far you figure we've come since leaving Karl?" James asked.

"Not sure," Agatha said, looking at the angle of the shadows cast from the scattered trees. "It's been almost an hour."

"I thought he would've caught up by now. Ain't like we're moving fast."

"You think we should head back a ways?" she asked.

"Maybe we can hold up when we reach those rocks up there," he said. "It'll give us the high ground so we can see."

"How about we hold up before that," she said. "To get to the peak, we have to go through the valley. And I have a bad feeling."

James nodded in agreement. They continued to ride for a spell in silence, and her thoughts went back to Hank. He hadn't answered her proposal. Maybe he wasn't interested after all. Maybe she'd gotten the wrong impression and her feelings for him ran deeper than his for her.

She was saved from her worry by a rustling in the forest in the distance. At first, she thought Karl had finally caught up with them, but before she could search for him she heard the thunderous trampling of hooves shaking the ground beneath them.

"Trouble," she said, clicking her tongue and snapping the reins of the wagon to move faster.

"I hear it," James said. "We need to take cover."

Agatha followed James to the edge of a wooded area. There weren't many spots with thickets of brush and trees, but they didn't have time to shop around. The rickety wagon's wooden seat jarred her body and rattled her teeth. She maneuvered with her left hand as she reached for her rifle.

"Aggie, wedge the wagon as deep into these trees as you can," James instructed.

"Don't call me Aggie."

"Hank calls you Aggie," James said.

"Yes, but I love him so he can get away with it."

Agatha eased the wagon as deep as she could in between two giant live oak trees. She knew there'd be no getting it out unless they dismantled it, but at the moment, her concern was to stay alive.

"Think it might be Hank and the crew?" James whispered.

Agatha shook her head. She knew it was the Copper Cove Boys. Somehow, she always knew she'd end up on the short end of the stick where they were concerned. She was willing to take on the fight to get them though. Good people had to start taking a stand against thugs like them.

"Should we move deeper into the brush?" Agatha asked.

The horses slowed, and she heard voices in the distance. Agatha and James weren't visible from the plains, but a decent tracker would have no problem finding them. Just the broken foliage from the wagon was enough to alert anyone.

"You ready?" James asked her.

She hesitated. Agatha had shot at a few people but she'd never actually shot anyone. "Yeah."

"I'd suggest we open fire as soon as they turn toward this direction. Otherwise, we'll give them time to split up."

She swallowed hard. "Okay."

"We can't hesitate on this," he insisted. "They'll adjust once they know we've hunkered down instead of running to hide."

"Think they know it's just us two?" Agatha asked.

"I'm sure of it," James replied.

She slid the rifle up and braced herself between the massive tree roots coming out of the ground.

"If we've gotta make a run for it, head straight back," James said. "That's the river behind us. Who knows? Maybe they can't swim."

She blinked and strained for any sign of movement. The Copper Cove Boys were coming in with the sun to their backs, so most of what she was seeing was mired in glare from the light.

She heard James moving further away from her. What was he doing? She'd never felt so alone as mysterious black silhouettes emerged in the dim spaces of shadow and light. They moved quickly and without sound. Like ghosts, each man would move and then disappear again.

It didn't take long to figure out their pattern, and she sucked in a breath and held it.

One...Two...Three...

Agatha pulled the trigger just as a man popped out from behind a tree, and he dropped to the ground. There was a shriek and a war cry before gunfire erupted all around her. She pressed tighter against the tree. It was obvious they didn't know where the shot came from. They were wasting ammunition trying to flush her out.

In the lull of rampage, she heard a single shot ring out. She knew it was James. A tree stump moved to her left and she realized it was a man, so she leveled the rifle and pulled the trigger.

"Got him," she muttered.

She tried to hurry up and reload, but her hands were shaking. She fought to hold them steady, but it was as though they had a life of their own.

"Calm down," she whispered over and over again. It hit her like a bolder that she had just killed two human beings. But this was no time to fall apart. They would surely find and kill her.

She flinched at the sound of more gunfire, and she fell backward when the sharp shards of the tree she'd been using for cover exploded around her. She scanned the area, but blood or sweat was dripping into her eyes, so she used her shirt to wipe it away.

Blood.

Agatha shivered as another shot was fired. This time

from James. Suddenly, a volley of shots echoed through the woods and she heard James yell and then collapse.

"No," she said, crawling on all fours to get to him. "Agatha Christie Harley, pull yourself together right now."

The crack of a fallen tree branch behind her had her freezing in place and fear snaking up her spine. She rolled to the right, but he was standing almost on top of her. Too close to point her rifle. He moved in quick, and she saw the knife lifted over his head, ready to strike.

Agatha shoved her hand inside of her coat pocket and yanked out a small .22 revolver that Hank had given her. Without looking or aiming, she pulled the trigger over and over again until it clicked empty. The man didn't stop coming.

She rolled just before the man's body collapsed next to her. He looked dead. Whether he was or not, she still had to survive. She fumbled with the revolver and tried to open the cylinder to reload it. She heard a rustle and realized the man was trying to push himself up. His face and torso were smeared with blood, but he still held the knife.

"No!" she screamed.

She closed her eyes and prayed, and then heard a mighty *whack*. And when she opened her eyes again she saw Karl standing over the man's body. He'd hit him with the butt of his rifle.

"You're okay," Karl said, crouching down beside her.

"James," she said. "He's shot."

Karl nodded. "Hold tight and keep your eyes open." And then he began to belly-crawl across an open area to look for James.

She had to keep an eye out while Karl attended to James. In all the commotion, she'd lost any perspective on where the killers might be. Still, she hunkered down and scanned back and forth.

"I think they're gone," Karl called out. "I heard the horses while you were trying to catch your breath."

She nodded and let herself relax a little. And then she heard the sound of horses again and the sweetest sound she'd ever heard.

"Agatha!" Hank called out.

The outlaws must've heard them coming. She collapsed against the tree. McIrish couldn't run forever.

CHAPTER EIGHT

Hank heaved himself against the wagon, but it didn't budge. It was wedged between two giant trees, and what had been a good strategy for keeping Agatha, James, and the horses safe during the Copper Cove Boys' ambush, had quickly become a challenge.

"Boss, you need help?" Springer asked.

Hank waved him off, though he could've used the help. But he didn't want anyone to see him so broken up with emotion over what could've happened to Agatha. He'd almost lost her, and the threat of the job was precisely why he hadn't asked her to marry him. Except now it wasn't a threat. It was real. Very real.

He knew she was safe now, and that Jason and James were attending to her. She'd gone into shock once her adrenaline had spiked and then bottomed out. Hank thought it was best to give her some space because he wasn't sure if he could hold his emotions in check. His gut told him to take off after McIrish and kill him. His head told him to stick with the team and rescue Coil.

He grunted as his boots slipped across the leaves, but he

was determined to get the wagon out and back on the trail to find his friend. It wouldn't be long before sundown, and they'd either have to bunk out in the open or press on into the darkness.

"Hey, Hank. Got a second?" Will asked.

"Not now."

"I think you're going to want to hear this."

Hank's heart pounded and he felt a surge of frustration. It wasn't really about the wagon. It was about his guilt over not being there to protect Agatha. He pulled the tattered leather gloves off finger by finger and tried his best to get himself under control before he turned to face his friend.

"Hear what?"

"That bandit that Karl knocked out is blabbering like a baby," Will said, jabbing a thumb over his shoulder. "You might want to hear this."

"Where'd all the blood come from?" Hank asked.

"Agatha shot him with the little .22 revolver you gave her. Put a couple of holes in him, but didn't do any real damage."

Hank hadn't taken any time to look at the man they'd taken prisoner, but as soon as he walked over to him, recognition hit.

"Jackson?" Hank asked.

"Yeah? So?" the big man asked.

"It's me. Marshal Hank Davidson."

"Hank?" Jackson asked. "What in the world are you doing here?"

"I could ask you the same thing," Hank said.

"I followed McIrish here to make a fresh start."

"You call this a fresh start?" Hank asked, incredulous. "Robbing and killing?"

"I had to get out of Philly," he said. "The military and the marshals were on my trail."

"You know this guy?" Karl asked.

"I arrested him after he went AWOL from military duty. He didn't want to serve time in the brig, so he gave me some information that led to solving a series of crimes just outside of New York."

"He's a cooperator," Will said.

"No, he's a snitch," Hank corrected.

"What's a snitch?" Karl asked.

"It's someone who helps law enforcement by giving information," Hank explained.

"Like I said," Will insisted. "A cooperator."

"Right," Hank said.

"Can you help an old pal out?" Jackson asked.

It took a minute for it to sink in before the reality of what Jackson had just tried to do slammed into him.

"You just tried to kill my fiancée," he said with a growl, clasping both hands around Jackson's thick neck.

"Hank," everyone seemed to say at once, and then they were pulling him away.

Hank stumbled backward. He was furious, and someone was going to pay. McIrish had destroyed so many lives in Hank's future, and was continuing to do so in his past. It was time to end the violence.

"Sorry, Hank," Jackson offered. "I didn't know she was yours."

Hank stared at the big man and wanted to hate him, but just like the times before, he saw a naivety in Jackson. Hank wasn't sure if it was because he knew of the horrors Jackson survived as an orphan, or that he wanted to see the good in people, but Jackson was one of those folks who made it hard to hate. He'd still be held accountable, but now wasn't the time. They needed to find Coil.

"Where's Coil?" Hank asked. "The Ranger McIrish shot the other day."

"Last time I saw him was after he got shot," Jackson said, wrinkling his nose. "That was probably a good ten miles west toward the army outpost."

"Did anyone try to find him after he was dismounted?"

"Naw, Dillon's a good shot," Jackson said. "If that Ranger fell, then he's dead."

"Even so, he still deserves to be recovered," Hank said. "Let's get this one up and into the wagon."

"You taking me with you?" Jackson asked.

"We sure aren't leaving you to run free," Hank said. "Of course, you know what they did to Cornbread when we captured him."

Jackson paled, and Hank hauled him to his feet.

"Pick better friends," Hank whispered to him. "And stay close. We might be the only chance you have."

James and Springer secured Jackson into the back of the wagon. It wasn't like McIrish to take a beating and retreat without preparing for a counterpunch. Hank knew it'd only be a matter of time before the gang was back. And with a prisoner in tow, they'd be at a disadvantage.

"Jackson said the last time he saw Coil was about ten miles west of the military outpost," Hank said. "As I figure it, that puts him closer to where we are now. I'd suggest we keep moving in the same direction in hopes of running into him."

"Coil is horseless," Whitehorse said. "He won't be caught walking along this trail. If it were me, I'd head to the river or to the train tracks. He's safer there, and it keeps him mostly hidden from the main routes back to San Antonio."

"You think he's heading back to San Antonio?" Will asked.

"It's home," Whitehorse said. "Coil would expect us to look for him, but at this point, he's not technically late. If it wasn't for his horse showing up without him, we'd have never known he was in trouble."

"Good thinking," Will said.

"How far are we from the train tracks?" Hank asked.

"We can be there before nightfall, but we gotta go east and cross the river. It gets narrow at the crossing up ahead."

"Okay," Hank agreed. "As soon as we free the wagon, we'll move out."

"It's already free, Boss," James said.

"What?" Hank asked. "How?"

"Jackson pushed it out for us. The man's a beast. No wonder those bullets didn't take him down."

"Don't forget that beast almost killed Agatha and is a ruthless outlaw," Karl warned. "Don't let your guard down."

Everyone nodded their heads in agreement as they looked beneath a patch of trees where Jackson sat humming in the sun. It had been an insane few hours, but the team was back together, and other than both Agatha and James taking superficial injuries from the gunfight, they were ready to find Coil.

Hank told Agatha to swap places with James, so he rode in the wagon and she was on horseback. James and Springer would fare better as wagon tenders while they kept an eye on Jackson. He put Agatha in between himself and Jason, who was at the lead. That left Will back in the rear guard post, but there was no one better at protecting against sudden ambush attacks.

Hank moved closer so he could see Agatha's profile. She was stunning in the setting sunlight. She'd taken a few licks in the gun battle, but the core of who she was shined though the blood smeared across her forehead and the mud caked in her hair. He couldn't wait for the right moment to pop the question.

"You okay?" she asked, noticing he'd been watching her.

"I'm fine. Why?"

"One of the boys mentioned they saw you crying in the woods."

"What?" Hank said, jerking back on the reins. "That's crazy." He quickly patted Beemer to apologize for the abrupt reaction.

"I'm just telling you what they said." She grinned mischievously.

"Who said it?" he asked.

"I ain't tell'n. I ain't no snitch," she said, using the word he'd introduced them to earlier.

"Nobody would say that about me."

"Suit yourself, tough guy," she said, chuckling. Agatha trotted up to where Jason was leading the convoy, so Hank eased back and rode next to Will.

"Did you say something to Aggie about me?"

"Oh no, partner," he said. "I ain't getting in in the middle of you two again."

"I said I was sorry the last time," Hank said.

"My friend, the fact that there was a last time is enough times to tell me to stay out of your affairs," Will said.

"I guess that's fair," Hank said. "But I figure you should know I'm going to pop the question as soon as I can."

"Out here?" Will asked, his brows raising in surprise.

"Why wait?" Hank asked. "And I thought you said you weren't interested."

Will laughed. "I never said I wasn't interested. I just know better than to meddle in your business."

LILIANA HART & LOUIS SCOTT

"Who's getting hitched?" Jackson asked from the wagon.

"Mind your own business," Will said.

Jackson shrugged and laid back down.

"What are we going to do with that one?" Will asked.

"Well, when we find Coil, there's only room for one in that wagon."

"And?"

Hank thought about it for a spell. "And I guess we'll figure it out when the time comes"

Hank noticed that Whitehorse had turned into a clearing beyond the trees. The rocks were directly ahead, and Hank figured that was the point of departure for making their way to the train tracks. He and Will decided to hang back a bit and try to cover up any signs of where they might've gone.

It wasn't long before they'd caught back up with the others as the wagon slowly traversed a bedrock river. The water wasn't rushing, but the debris and uneven surface were giving them fits. Springer looked capable, but the extra heft of Jackson had offset the center of gravity. Agatha was already out of the water and onto the opposite shore while Whitehorse came back to help with the wagon.

The back wheel caught a rock and teetered back and forth, and then the whole wagon started to tilt.

"We're tipping," James yelled out.

"Cut him loose," Will hollered.

It was obvious from their vantage point that Jackson's size had become too unstable for the rickety wagon. Freeing him was the only way to save the wagon and keep Jackson from drowning.

"Don't free him," Agatha shouted.

"Gotta do it," James said, hacking through the ropes that

bound up the big outlaw.

Jackson dropped into the water, and immediately the wagon stabilized and the horses were able to right themselves against an increasing current. James and Springer hustled to keep the supplies from being ruined, but there was nothing they could do about Jackson.

For a big man, he sure moved fast through the water.

Hank watched as Agatha leveled her rifle.

"No!" Hank yelled.

"He's escaping!"

"Too loud," Hank replied. "Your shot will draw attention."

He watched as she fought an inner battle and finally lowered the weapon. She shoved the rifle back into its leather sleeve with a huff. Then she reached down on the other side of her saddle and came up with something new.

"Is that a bow and arrow?" Hank asked.

Will started laughing. "That's what it looks like."

"Jackson," Hank yelled. "You better stop."

The bear of a man looked like he was starting to tucker out as his water sprint morphed into a trudge. Even so, he was still putting space between them and him.

"Well, I tried to warn you," Hank said quietly.

"Think we should stop her?" Will asked.

"Do you think we *could* stop her?" he asked.

Both men watched in awe as Agatha drew back on the bow and unleashed an arrow toward Jackson. He screamed out loud as the arrow sunk into the back of his hamstring. It wasn't a fatal shot, but the way he was thrashing in the water would've said otherwise.

Agatha turned toward Hank and gave him a thumbs up.

"Are you sure you want to marry her?" Will asked.

"Oh, yeah," Hank said. "Definitely."

CHAPTER NINE

It had been one long and exhausting day.

Their task had seemed simple at the time. All they needed was to find Coil and bring him home—dead or alive. But somehow, they'd ended up chasing a stagecoach, surviving a gun battle, and almost getting swept away by the river. Not to mention she'd killed a couple of men, and shot another with her bow. And though Agatha would never admit it, she'd actually been aiming for his buttocks.

They'd agreed to change their course and head away from the military outpost and toward the railroad tracks, traveling in between the tracks and the river. Logic had dictated that route was probably the one Coil had taken if he'd managed to survive. Since they knew Coil's time could be limited, and the fact that they'd picked up their slightly worse for wear prisoner thanks to Agatha, bedding down for the night wasn't an option.

It was a shade past dusk, and a full moon and star-filled sky helped them navigate their way along a rocky ledge that was expected to set them very close to the Union Pacific Railroad track. Temperatures had turned cold as soon as night had fallen, and Agatha was glad for the wool-lined coat and gloves she wore. The cold was making her clumsy, and she was long past exhaustion.

Agatha knew how to prepare for the changing elements, but it didn't mean she enjoyed the drastic drop in temperature. She liked her creature comforts—like a bed, a fire, and hot tea. She nestled her gloved hand through the bulk of layered clothing until she felt a stick of beef jerky. She gnawed on it, feeling the salt course through her veins, and tried to ignore her growling stomach. It would have to do for dinner.

She'd lived a life on the edge. It was a life she'd never once apologized for, but at times, she did wonder what it would have been like on the other side. If she'd been a "normal" lady of gentle breeding. If she'd settled down and married, raised a family, and tended to hearth and home.

Her father had always told her she'd been a late bloomer, but sometimes the flowers that took the longest to bloom were the most beautiful. She didn't regret her life. And she was glad she'd waited because she'd found Hank, and she knew he was meant for her. But something was holding him back. And all she could reason was that it was her. Maybe she wasn't feminine enough. Maybe she embarrassed him.

One thing she knew for sure was that she wouldn't wait around for him forever. She had too much self-respect for that.

"Hey, Aggie," Hank said, surprising her. "Nice shot, pretty lady."

She laughed. She couldn't help herself. He was always making her laugh.

"Thank you," she said, primly. "I like having a few surprises up my sleeve. I'm like a little Cupid."

"Well, I hope you only have arrows for me," Hank teased.

"You know I do," she said, batting her eyes. It always worked for the girls back home. Maybe she just needed to flirt more for him to get the hint. "How would you like me to shoot you with one?"

Hank barked out a laugh, and she felt the heat of embarrassment in her face.

"Like poor Jackson?" he asked. "No, thank you."

Agatha pursed her lips and tugged on Jeep's reins, creating a gap between her and Hank. So she didn't know how to flirt. So what? He didn't have to laugh at her. The stupid man.

Hank reached across the gap and grabbed her reins, pulling her back toward him.

"Hey, Aggie," he said in a whisper. "I'd like to talk with you at some point about our future."

"Our future?" she asked, butterflies dancing in her stomach.

"Yes. Our future. Together."

"Are you a fortune teller then?" she asked

"More than you know," he mumbled.

She watched him shift uncomfortably in his saddle. Hank wasn't the best when it came to talking about emotions.

"What was that?" she asked.

"You know what I'm saying," he said, blowing out a breath. "Don't make me spell it out."

"Spell what out?"

"You know," he said, gesturing with his hands. "The future."

"And what do you see in the future, Hank the fortune teller?" she asked.

"You wouldn't believe it if I told you," he said.

"Try me."

"Aggie, I love you and I want us to be together."

Her heart stuttered in her chest. "Are you asking me to marry you?"

"Not right this minute. It's so dark I wouldn't know if you were shaking you're head yes or no," he said. "I want to do it proper."

"Who are you going to ask for my hand?" she asked. "You know my folks have passed on. Will you get down on one knee? You know how your knees hurt when you've been down on the ground too long. You really should be careful. I'd like to travel someday. Maybe out to San Francisco or New York. There's a lot of world to see."

Agatha knew she was rambling, but she couldn't make herself stop talking. She'd thought about the reality of them marrying, and even assumed she'd be rational about the whole process, but she had no idea how excited she'd be when it began to happen.

"You're asking a lot of questions," Hank said, chuckling. "You might want to give yourself some time to breathe."

"Sorry," she said, but her smile said she was anything but. She suddenly felt flushed with heat, love, excitement and embarrassment, all at the same time. What didn't help were the thick bundles of clothing she'd donned for their night ride. Her skin was burning hot, but there wasn't anything she could do about it.

She closed her eyes and thought about their wedding day. She didn't have any family left, so it'd be a small affair, but it didn't matter. All that mattered was she'd get to call Hank her husband at the end of it. She hadn't realized marriage had been a secret dream until she'd let it become a reality.

Between the exhaustion, the excitement, the swaying of her body back and forth in the saddle, and the fact that she'd closed her eyes, she must've lulled herself to sleep because the next thing she knew she was sliding off of Jeep onto the cold hard ground.

"Agatha?" Hank asked, patting her cheek. "You okay?"

Agatha slowly opened her eyes. The stars were beautiful. And then she saw several worried faces looking down at her.

"What happened?" she asked.

"I think you fell asleep," Hank said.

"It's been a long day," she said. "I'm okay."

"I didn't know talk of our future would put you to sleep," Hank teased.

"Why?" Will asked. "It put the rest of us to sleep. You two sure do talk loud."

"Yeah," James said. "Just marry the woman already."

Agatha felt her face heating even more and rolled to her hands and knees to get up. Hank was there to help her, lifting her to her feet, and holding her loosely in his arms until she was steady on her feet.

"Thanks," Agatha said softly, leaning her head against his shoulder.

"Did they get married yet?" Jackson called out from the wagon.

"Nope," Springer said.

"Too bad," Jackson said. "I love weddings."

"Good grief," Agatha said. "This is ridiculous."

"Maybe this is a good time to regroup," Will said. "We can grab some quick chow and some shuteye."

"But no fires," James said, reminding everyone.

Agatha figured after her last stunt she needed a break. But she wasn't too keen on doing without the fire, though she wouldn't complain. In her experience, people who complained didn't get invited on adventures. And if she could put something in her stomach other than jerky, she'd be grateful.

Her backside was sore from the saddle, and she stretched her muscles. Exhaustion overtook her and she barely glanced at the others as they dug out the food. She made herself as comfortable a pallet as she could and curled up to go to sleep.

"Agatha," Hank said.

It sounded like he was talking through water, and she shrugged him off. Then she heard her name again. And again. Hank sure was becoming a nuisance. They'd have to do something about that after they got married.

"What?" she snarled.

"We gotta move," Hank said.

Agatha sat straight up, almost butting Hank in the head. She'd been sleeping hard. "What happened? Did the Copper Cove Boys find us? Did Jackson escape again?"

"Relax," Hank said. He pointed to Jackson leaning against the wagon wheel. "Whitehorse thinks he sees something. It might be Coil."

She rubbed her eyes and tried to slap some color in her cheeks and wake up a bit. And then she scrambled to her feet, rolling up her bedroll and wool blanket.

"Wait a second," she said. "What could Whitehorse possibly see? It's dark out here."

"The moon is bright tonight," Hank said. "And Whitehorse said he saw a reverse smoke signal drifting from behind the ledges that overlook the train tracks."

"What's a reverse smoke signal?" she asked.

"It comes from a Dakota fire hole," Hank said. "It's an underground fire to keep anyone from seeing the flames. It burns hot and creates a different kind smoke. It has to be Coil. There's not too many people who would know about that."

"Impressive," she said. "Let's get moving."

Hank held her by the shoulders. "Whoa, hold on," he said. "We can't just stroll up to the fire. That's a good way to die. There's no telling who it might be, and if it is Coil, you can bet he'll come out fighting."

"You're right," she said. "Can't we just call out to him?"

"What if it's McIrish and the gang laying a trap?" Hank asked.

"Then we finish him off," she said. "It's what he deserves. We can take them."

"Hold on, tiger," Hank said. "How about we focus on Coil first and then we'll worry about finishing off McIrish?"

"Deal," she said, giving him a quick kiss. "But I'm going to hold you to it."

"Are you sure they didn't get married?" Jackson asked, watching them closely.

"We did *not* get married," Agatha said.

"Yet," Hank clarified.

"So what's the plan?" she asked.

"You stay here and try to get some more sleep," Hank said. "Whitehorse knows this land like the back of his hand, and we're going to go check it out."

"You woke me up to tell me you were leaving me here?" she asked, aggravated.

"Well, yeah," he said, shrugging. "I guess so. And I wanted to tell you bye."

"Oh," she said, giving him another squeeze. "That's okay then. Be careful. And wake me up when you get back."

"Will do," he said. "Get some rest. You're going to need it."

"You don't have to tell me twice," she said, unrolling her bedding again, and crawling under the covers. She'd gotten cold again, and it was hard to warm up. She wished Hank was able to snuggle close and share his body heat, but she was jumping the gun. Wedding first, body heat later.

It wasn't long before she was being shaken awake once again, and someone was calling her name. She woke up easier this time, having never fully gotten warm or done more than doze on and off.

"What happened?" she asked. Hank's face was close to hers. "Any news?"

"We've got Coil," he said.

"No kidding?" she asked, coming to her feet. "That's incredible. How is he?"

"He's fine," Coil said, coming into view. He looked worn down and ragged, but there was a smile on his face. "Thanks for asking."

Agatha was so relieved to see that he was safe, she wrapped her arms around his neck and hugged him.

"Shelly's going to be so happy to see you," Agatha said. "If she doesn't kill you first."

Coil snorted out a laugh, and winced, grabbing his midsection.

"Are you hurt?"

"Just some bruised ribs," he said. "Maybe a crack or two."

"You're not shot?" she asked.

"Nope," he said. "McIrish's shot got close enough to my horse to spook him, and he threw me right in the nick of time, because I would've been filled with lead otherwise. My spur got caught on the way down and I got dragged through some pretty tough terrain. That's where I hurt my ribs." He'd noticed the big bear of a man by the wagon. "Is that Jackson?"

"In the flesh," Hank said.

"And what's that about?" Coil asked.

"Same old, same old," Agatha said. "Jackson tried to kill me, and then I shot him in the leg with an arrow. He's my prisoner."

"Your prisoner?" Coil asked, rubbing his hands over his eyes in disbelief. "Maybe I'm dead. None of this makes sense."

"Makes sense to me," Agatha said.

"And what are you going to do with your prisoner?"

"Have him stuffed and mounted to the wall, of course," she said. "I've decided to redecorate."

"You're a strange woman, Agatha Harley," Coil said.

"What happened with McIrish?" Hank asked.

"I knew he had something up his sleeve as soon as we set out for Austin. I figured it was an ambush, and once I saw what I was facing, I made my own plans. I was outnumbered and figured the smart thing to do was let them get away with it. And then I could gather up a posse and track them to their next town."

"But where did the blood come from on the saddle?" Agatha asked.

"I killed some rabbits our first night out for dinner, and I just hadn't cleaned the saddle," Coil said. "Didn't mean to give y'all a fright."

"Well, Coil," Hank said. "It looks like you've got your posse. Let's go round up the Copper Cove Boys."

CHAPTER TEN

It was February sixteenth, and the morning was crisp and clear. Hank had been in 1874 for three days. How and why he was there was still a mystery, but one fact he'd come to accept was that this wasn't a dream. He'd never had a dream this real, where he could taste, touch, and smell everything around him. Where the realities of love, loss and life all hung in the balance.

Dawn lazily approached and fingers of orange and yellow crept across the horizon, and they'd waited until light touched the sky to start a fire. The coffee was strong, and the last dregs heated over a waning fire as they discussed their strategy for capturing Dillon McIrish and his rebel band of marauders. Everyone except Agatha. She'd been plum tuckered out, and no one had the heart to wake her. Or maybe everyone was too afraid to wake her. She wasn't a morning person.

Coil had been doing most of the talking. After the Copper Cove Boys had thought him dead, they'd set up camp near the place Coil had been thrown from his horse so McIrish could tend to his own wounds. He'd gotten roughed up pretty good in the scuffle that had led to his arrest. Coil's horse had long taken off, but he'd made himself a ghost in the woods close enough to hear the gang plotting their next heist. He knew every detail. And it was going to be their downfall.

"What are they planning?" Springer asked. "Another bank robbery?"

"Nope," Coil said, drinking coffee from his tin cup. "A train robbery."

"A train?" Will asked. "There's nothing but coal and supply trains around here. Why would they want to rob a train?"

Coil was already shaking his head. "Not this time," he said. "There's a private train scheduled to come all the way from Dallas. No passengers. But they've disguised the cars to look like a cargo train, though all of the cars will have an armed guard inside, and they're the only ones who can unlock their car."

"And what's inside the cars that the Copper Cove Boys want so bad?" Hank asked.

"Gold bars," Coil answered. "Worth at least a million."

Whitehorse whistled.

"They had the train schedule and the route, and the train is only scheduled to stop twice for a minute in each place to take on water. It's timed down to the second. The train will make its final stop in San Antonio where it will be met by armed guards and men strong enough to move that many crates of gold bars."

"How are they planning on getting the gold off the train?" James asked.

"They're not," Coil said. "They're planning to take control of the whole train and divert it down a different section of tracks. They'll kill the guards, and unload the gold at Canyon Springs. They've got a hideout near there. If they pull it off as planned, the train will get back on the right track and pull into the station in San Antonio with nothing but a bunch of dead guards and empty cars."

"When are they going to strike?" Hank asked.

Coil sighed and looked them each in the eye. "Today."

Hank's eyes widened. "What do you mean today?"

"I mean there's one shot at keeping them from succeeding in their plan." Coil said. "We need to be in the right place at the right time. And I need to be on that train when it comes through."

"You mean we're *all* going to be on that train when it comes through," Agatha said.

Hank had been so engrossed in Coils's story that he hadn't heard her come up behind them.

"Good morning, Aggie," he said, wondering if she thought he'd left her out of the loop on purpose.

"Morning, Hank," she said, nodding. She looked in the kettle to see if there was any more coffee, and poured the rest into her cup. "I'm sure it was just an oversight to leave me sleeping while the menfolk planned things out."

Will jerked his head over toward Jackson, who continued to snore next to the wagon. "You're not the only one."

She got a mutinous look on her face, and Hank stifled a grin. He knew that look well, and Will's best course of action was to stop talking.

"I think Aggie's right," Hank said. "It's going to take all of us to stop them. We all need to be on that train. It's the only way to protect the cargo."

Coil nodded and said, "Normally, I'd agree with you. But the reality is, we have a prisoner, several horses, and a wagon that have to be tended to and taken back to town."

Hank gestured for Agatha to take a seat next to him on the fallen log he was using as a bench. She looked like she might protest, but she sat and then said, "If that's the case, that leaves me out. I can't babysit a killer all the way back to San Antonio. It's got to be a lawman."

"Then who's gonna take him back?" Hank asked.

Springer raised his hand. "I'll do it. I know manpower is limited, and I can run that wagon and horse team better than two of us could. If Jackson gives me any grief, I'll shoot him in the other leg. But I plan on keeping him restrained for the journey home. And he won't have anyone to rescue him with the great train robbery going on."

"You sure?" Hank asked, surprised the younger man wanted to miss out on the action.

"I'm sure," he said. "Besides, anytime I'm on a train or a boat I'm sick as a dog. Don't think you want to deal with that."

"Good point," Coil said. "Now that we've got that planned, we need to go over the logistics. I think I've pinpointed the perfect spot for us to join the party. It's a good place for us to board because the train has to slow down before several switchbacks."

"What if the Copper Cove Boys are also planning to board at the same place?" Whitehorse asked.

Coil shook his head. "I don't think so. I think they'll shoot for when the train has a planned stop."

Hank's gut knotted. How in the world were they all going to get on a moving train, even if it did slow down? The last time Hank had hitched a ride on a train like that, he'd been a kid back in Philly.

Coil used his fingers to push his long blonde hair back from his face. "We'll only have one shot to get on. There's a ravine not too far past that point, and the drop would kill anyone."

"How are we supposed to jump on a moving train?" James asked.

"Why don't we use the wagon?" Whitehorse suggested. "It'll hold at least a couple of us and we can make a jump for it. It's a lot easier than jumping off a horse. Believe me."

"That wagon can't get us up to speed," James said. "We'd be lucky if it didn't fall apart right out from under us."

Agatha looked thoughtful. "We just need it to last long enough to get us onto the train. If we hitch all four horses to it, we can get some serious speed."

Hank had been listening to the conversation with one ear, but he was watching Coil. He seemed detached. He knew his friend well enough to recognize the rage that simmered inside of him. Coil had been the one whose life had been threatened. And he wanted revenge. He wouldn't have given a hoot who made it on the train as long as he was the one to face off with McIrish.

"Y'all can plan this to death," Coil said. But that train is going to be coming through in a couple of hours, and wagon or no wagon, I'm going to meet it." He stood and went to ready his things.

It didn't take long for them to clear their camp and mount their horses, and they were on their way to the spot where they'd attempt to jump on the train as it passed by. It was decided Springer would drive the wagon since he and Jackson were splitting off toward home, and they'd hitched up four horses and dumped all of their supplies to lighten the load. It was also decided that Jackson would remain tied to a tree with the supplies and one of the horses that was older and wouldn't have the stamina for this mission.

Springer would swing back and get him once he'd delivered them to the train.

"Do you think this will work?" Agatha asked him.

"I'm not sure," Hank answered honestly. "What are the chances of catching a moving locomotive in an old wagon filled with people?"

"If we get a head start and get it up to speed, we might have a chance," James said.

"How fast do you think we've got to go?" Agatha asked.

"Eighty-eight miles per hour," Hank said under his breath, *Back to the Future* immediately coming to mind.

"What's that?" Agatha asked.

"Nothing," Hank said. "Come on. Let's get this thing moving before the team goes on without us."

Springer hopped up into the front, and Hank and Agatha got settled in the back They met the others at the crest of the hill where they'd decided to strap down Jackson and the equipment they didn't need at the moment. Coil, Whitehorse, and Ellis decided to forego the wagon and jump from their horses onto the train. The lighter they could make the wagon, the better chance they had.

Just to the north of where they'd stashed Jackson was a hill that looked out over the valley where the tracks had been laid. They were at an incline, and would be able to see the train as it slowed and came around the bend.

Waiting was always the hardest part. His breakfast sat in his gut like lead as he waited to see the first sign of the train.

"You okay?" Agatha asked.

"Never better," he said. "You?"

"I'm ready," she said, shaking out arms and stretching her neck like she was about to go into the ring.

"Y'all are both crazy," James said, shaking his head.

"We're about to jump on a moving train and confront the most notorious gang in the country."

"It'll be fun," Hank said, ignoring his own nerves to calm James. He looked a little green around the gills. "And it'll be a good story to tell your grandkids one day."

James snorted. "Yeah, if we live to tell the tale."

"That's the whistle," Agatha said, and everyone froze. It was faint, but it was there.

His heart pounded in his chest and he gripped the side of the wagon.

"It's all about timing," Coil said. "We need to start moving before we see the train. Otherwise we'll never get the speed we need."

There was another blow of the whistle, closer this time. The horses pawed the ground in anticipation, and the excitement was electric. The next whistle was the signal, and with a mighty, "Yah!" the horses were all spurred into action.

The wagon jerked beneath them as the team took off, and Hank braced himself as they started down the hill. His teeth rattled in his head, and he kept an eye on Agatha to make sure she was okay.

"Here she comes," Agatha yelled over the thundering of hooves.

He saw the black smoke first, and then the whistle sounded again. And then the train appeared, looking intimidating and larger than life as it barreled toward them. They must be out of their minds, but it was too late for regrets now.

They were all riding at a break-neck pace along the tracks, and the train would come up beside them in a matter of seconds. He caught a glimpse of the engineer's wide-eyed stare as the locomotive passed them.

The clack of the train hitting the tracks was like a metronome in his ears, and his gaze scanned for the best place to take hold.

"Dang it," Agatha yelled. "I dropped my rifle."

Hank glanced back and realized that was the least of their problems. The wagon was coming apart at the seams, and then they'd be in a real fix.

"We gotta make the jump," he said. "Keep it steady, Springer."

"The middle rail car is open," Hank said. "That's our easiest point of entry."

"You call that easy?" Agatha asked.

They'd be even with the empty car in seconds, and Hank knew jumping into the car wouldn't be as difficult as it would be to stop themselves from rolling out the other side.

"James," Hank said. "You jump first. Then you can catch Agatha."

Hank took a second to glance at the riders behind them, trying to find their own place to jump on, but the train had started picking up speed again and things weren't looking good. He couldn't think about that now. He had to focus on getting on that train.

The ride was getting rougher as the wagon splintered apart, and they hit a rut in the road that had them going airborne. Hank heard a yell, and looked back in time to see Springer bounce right out of the wagon.

He'd never seen anything like it. "What the—"

"He's fine," James yelled, leaping into the drivers' seat and taking the reins. He snapped them to keep the horses from slowing their pace.

"It'll have to be just us," Agatha said. "It's now or never. Toss me."

Hank didn't take the time to think it through. He picked Agatha up and tossed her into the open car on the train. Coil and the others on horses had missed their opportunity when they'd had to dodge Springer, and the pieces of the wagon that had come flying at them.

With a mighty leap, Hank launched himself into the open car and his fingers grasped a crate to keep him from rolling out the other side. The train whistle blared once more, and it was then Hank realized the enormity of their problem. He and Agatha were truly alone. It was going to be them and the Copper Cove Boys. And he wasn't thrilled with their odds of coming out on top.

CHAPTER ELEVEN

"Wow," Agatha said. "That went a lot different in my head."

Hank was sprawled on hands and knees, trying to catch his breath instead of staring at how close he'd come to the drop-off on the other side of the car. He scooted back across the filthy floor and pressed his back against the wall, taking in deep heaving breaths.

"You okay?" he asked Agatha.

"Just dandy," she said. But there was something in the tone of her voice that had him glancing at her. She was pale, and her mouth was pinched with pain.

He rose to his feet and braced himself, trying to find the rhythm of the train before taking a step.

"What's wrong? He asked, moving toward her.

"Nothing," she insisted.

But he'd already noticed she was favoring her shoulder, and there was definitely something wrong with it. It was dislocated.

"No, you're definitely not all right," he said.

"I think I'm going to be sick," she said, and then her eyes

rolled back in her head and he barely caught her as she passed out cold.

There were several empty crates stacked at each end, and several of them had remnants of hay that had been used in the packing. He laid her carefully in the corner and then rearranged the crates so she'd be protected.

"And then there was one," Hank said to himself.

The train whistle blew again, and it began to slow. He knew it wouldn't be long before they arrived at the switchbacks, and that was the mostly likely moment for McIrish to make his move.

There was a squeal of brakes, and he braced himself against the wall as the train slowed even more. He poked his head out and looked both ways. He didn't recognize the area, and the only thing he had to go by was Coil's description of the switchbacks, a deep ravine, and a canyon once they'd diverted the train.

He saw the plumes of dust and heard the gunfire as they shot off rounds into the air. The security guards would all be tucked safely into the individual cars where the gold was located, and they'd put up a fight to protect it.

The gunfire stopped as abruptly as it started, and Hank just listened. He checked on Agatha one more time, and then he waited, anticipation curling through him.

There was a thud on the roof of the car, and then the sound of footsteps. He reached for his pistol, and took cover behind one of the crates. The element of surprise would only work once.

Hank saw the boots first, and then a large man swung into the car from above. He recognized the man from one of Agatha's in depth articles and the likenesses she'd printed of each gang member. The man was known as skunk because of the distinctive white stripe that ran through his black hair.

Skunk gave the car a cursory look and then stuck his head out into the open and yelled for the others. The easy thing to do would be to shoot him where he stood, but Hank couldn't stand the thought of shooting a man in the back. He put his pistol back in the holster and picked up a section of 2x4 that was next to his feet.

He crept forward slowly and whacked him right across the backside and out of the train car. Skunk gave a muffled *mmpphh* and never saw what hit him. There was a shout and a volley of gunfire that hit the outside of the car Hank was in, and wood splintered all around him. He scrambled back into the corner where Agatha was, protecting her from flying debris.

He'd made someone very unhappy. The shots stopped and he tried to crawl back toward the opening to see who or how many were coming for him. He spotted another outlaw out of his periphery riding his horse at a breakneck pace to catch up. He couldn't identify the man on horseback because his Stetson covered too much of his face, but Hank recognized the pistol in his hand.

Hank drew his revolver and laid flat on the floor of the train car, and then took aim at the moving target. The gunshot echoed in the small space so it rang in his ears, but his aim was true. The horseman tumbled to the ground like a ragdoll.

He didn't know how many of McIrish's gang were left. The gang had killed Cornbread themselves, and Agatha and James had taken care of a small handful of miscreants when they'd had their shootout. Jackson had been captured, and Hank had just disposed of two. If his calculations were correct, that meant McIrish was the last man standing.

Even as he had the thought he heard the thump of footsteps and a jarring whack to the back of his head. He saw stars and went forward, his gun falling from his grasp and bouncing out of the open door.

He moaned as he fought to roll onto his side. The blurry shadow standing in the opposite doorway hovered over him. He'd used the same 2x4 Hank had whacked Skunk with.

"Well, well, well," McIrish drawled. "If it isn't Hammering Hank Davidson in the flesh. You've gotten good at looking in the wrong direction and letting someone sneak up behind you."

"What are you talking about?"

"The bank job in Philly," he said. "You and your misfits were watching the wrong bank. I tried to warn you, but the hotshot detective thought he knew better than the very man who planned the job."

"You tried to warn me?" Hank asked, confused. He was in pain. That blow might've cracked his skull. He already had damage from the horse kick to the head, and now he might have brain injuries that no doctor could fix if he got stuck in this time period. Coldness swept over his body, and he thought he might lose consciousness, but that would be the end for him and Agatha too. He had to fight.

"I didn't want them old guards to go down," McIrish said. "I'm not completely heartless, you know. Killing was never in the plan, only the money, but when people got in our way they left us no choice. But I did try to warn you. You could've saved those men, so really, it's your fault we had to kill them."

"You're wrong," Hank said, trying to get to his feet. "You're a killer, and nothing you say or do will ever erase the blood on your hands. You're a monster."

McIrish drove his foot deep into Hank's gut, and Hank

curled into a knot on the floor. Every click and clack of the train jarred his aching body, and he sucked in a deep breath, trying to control the pain.

"You didn't care about those innocent men," Hank said. "You've never cared about anyone but yourself. They had families. They weren't even armed."

"You get paid to put on a uniform, then you better be ready to fight for whatever it is that matters to you," McIrish said. "They knew the risk."

Something in what he'd said snapped Hank back into reality. He loved Agatha, and if he was going to keep his promise to protect her, he'd needed to fight for her.

McIrish slammed the 2x4 into Hank's shin, and something cracked. It was now or never. He wasn't going to lay down and die for a man like McIrish.

"I'm going to stop you," Hank said, preparing to launch himself.

"Really?" McIrish said, his laugh pure evil. "Like you were going to stop me back east? The only thing that stopped you then was a crooked politician. I could've done anything I wanted and gotten away with it. How does it feel to be a puppet? Senator Coglin told you to stop the investigation after that last robbery. That we'd gone underground and it was a waste of time, money, and manpower. How do you think he knew when went underground?"

Hank tried to compute. Coglin wasn't from the past. Coglin was the one who'd screwed up his investigation in the future. But it made sense. Hank hadn't thought about there being someone on the inside.

"I had no choice," Hank said, knowing he hadn't. "You can say what you want, but I had no authority to pursue you. I don't operate outside of the law. And maybe you got away then, but men like you always get what's coming to them."

McIrish laughed. "You're a fool Hank Davidson. Men like me always get exactly what they want in life. Where are you now? You lost your wife and gave up everything," he taunted. "And then you get a second chance at love and you're going to screw this up too. It doesn't seem to matter what time period you're in. You're a coward."

Hank shook his head, hoping to unscramble his brains. Did McIrish know he was from the future? What was happening? Maybe it was the brain damage, but nothing was making sense.

"This is crazy," Hank said.

"Is it?" McIrish taunted. "Agatha has been wanting to marry you for almost a hundred and fifty years, and you still haven't got it right. It doesn't matter though. I'll kill her before I kill you. Just so you can watch. You like watching your women die, don't you? You hid her behind that crate there, but she's hurt pretty bad. That takes some of the fun out of it. I want to be the one to cause the hurt. I'm going to haunt you in every life you live."

Anger fueled Hank like nothing ever had. It coursed through his body, and acted like a pain killer.

McIrish moved to hit him with the 2x4 again, and Hank rolled toward the middle of the boxcar so it missed him by inches. He swept out his leg into the back of McIrish's knees, using a little modern day Jiu Jitsu, and brought him to his knees so they were on a level playing field.

From that point on it was street fighting at its finest. Fists and feet connected with flesh, and blood flew and ribs and noses crunched beneath the force of well placed punches.

They were evenly matched and at a draw, and McIrish

must have come to the same conclusion because he rolled out of the way and reached for the board again. Hank made a split second decision and launched himself at McIrish's middle, pushing the man to the other side of the car and out the open door. Hank let go at the last second and grabbed hold of a metal rung before sending them both to their deaths.

But McIrish didn't fall how he'd planned. He clung to Hank's leg and dangled over the ravine they were crossing. Hank looked down and saw true fear in the man's eyes, and then he saw him reach for the Bowie knife hidden in his boot.

"Die!" screamed McIrish.

Hank acted on instinct and swung his free leg so it connected with McIrish's face. Blood and sweat dripped into Hank's eyes, and he couldn't see. Blood rushed in his ears. But he kept kicking, survival mode taking over.

"Hank," McIrish said.

The calmness of his voice made Hank freeze. There was something odd about it. Something out of place. He tried to clear his head and his eyes and look down at McIrish.

"You're getting a second chance," McIrish said. "Don't screw this one up."

"I don't understand," Hank said.

"You will." And then McIrish let go and fell into the blackness of the ravine. All Hank could do was watch until he disappeared for good.

His hands slipped on the metal rung he held onto, and he used every ounce of strength he had left to pull himself back into the boxcar. He crawled around the crates until he saw Agatha, safe and unconscious. He curled up next to her not knowing where they were going, but he didn't care because they were together and alive. And the bad guys had lost.

"Hank."

Something trickled across his forehead and he thought it might be blood.

"Hank."

This time he felt a light pat against his cheek, and he groaned in pain. He couldn't be dead. There wasn't supposed to be pain in death.

"Hank, wake up," Agatha said.

His eyes cracked open, and he was surprised they weren't swollen shut. That fight with McIrish had been a doozy.

"Hank," Agatha said again.

He smiled and tried to bring her into focus. She was so beautiful.

"We won," he said, bringing his hand up to push her hair back from her face.

"What did we win?"

"The fight. We beat the Copper Cove Boys once and for all."

She raised her brows, looking concerned. "Okay, baby. Are you hurt? One minute we were eating and the next you were passed out cold on the floor. The champagne cork conked you right in the head."

"Bessie kicked me in the head," he said, drowsily. But his brains were starting to put things to rights. Not Bessie. It had been a cork.

He looked around slowly and recognized the restaurant. He was back. He was alive. And so was Agatha. It had all been a dream.

"I've waited a hundred and fifty years to ask you this,"

he said, not caring that they'd drawn a crowd after his episode. "Agatha Harley, will you marry me?"

Her eyes widened in surprise. "Are you sure that's not the cork talking?"

"I've never been more sure of anything in my life," he said. "I love you. Without fear and without reservation. I want to spend the rest of my life with you."

A single tear slipped down her cheek and she leaned down to kiss him. "Yes, I'll marry you," she whispered.

"I've got a ring box in my pocket," he said.

"You can give it to me over dessert," she said. "They've comped our meal. They feel real bad about what happened to you. Besides, I want to hear all about the Copper Cove Boys. That sounds like a story I might want to write someday."

Hank laughed. "You wouldn't believe me if I told you."

NEXT UP: A SALT AND BATTERY

JUNE 2020

ORDER TODAY

Liliana and I have loved sharing these stories in our Harley & Davidson Mystery Series with you.

There are many more adventures to be had for Aggie and Hank. Make sure you stay up to date with life in Rusty Gun, Texas by signing up for our emails.

Thanks again and please be sure to leave a review where you bought each story and, recommend the series to your friends.

Kindly,
Scott & Liliana

Enjoy this book? You can make a big difference

Reviews are so important in helping us get the word out about Harley and Davidson Mystery Series. If you've enjoyed this adventure Liliana & I would be so grateful if you would take a few minutes to leave a review (it can be as short as you like) on the book's buy page.

Thanks,
Scott & Liliana

ALSO BY LILIANA HART

The MacKenzies of Montana

Dane's Return

Thomas's Vow

Riley's Sanctuary

Cooper's Promise

Grant's Christmas Wish

The MacKenzies Boxset

MacKenzie Security Series

Seduction and Sapphires

Shadows and Silk

Secrets and Satin

Sins and Scarlet Lace

Sizzle

Crave

Trouble Maker

Scorch

MacKenzie Security Omnibus 1

MacKenzie Security Omnibus 2

JJ Graves Mystery Series

Dirty Little Secrets

A Dirty Shame

Dirty Rotten Scoundrel

Down and Dirty

Dirty Deeds

Dirty Laundry

Dirty Money

A Dirty Job

Addison Holmes Mystery Series

Whiskey Rebellion

Whiskey Sour

Whiskey For Breakfast

Whiskey, You're The Devil

Whiskey on the Rocks

Whiskey Tango Foxtrot

Whiskey and Gunpowder

Books by Liliana Hart and Scott Silverii

The Harley and Davidson Mystery Series

The Farmer's Slaughter

A Tisket a Casket

I Saw Mommy Killing Santa Claus

Get Your Murder Running

Deceased and Desist

Malice In Wonderland

Tequila Mockingbird

Gone With the Sin

The Gravediggers

The Darkest Corner

Gone to Dust

Say No More

Lawmen of Surrender (MacKenzies-1001 Dark Nights)

1001 Dark Nights: Captured in Surrender

1001 Dark Nights: The Promise of Surrender

Sweet Surrender

Dawn of Surrender

The MacKenzie World (read in any order)

Trouble Maker

Bullet Proof

Deep Trouble

Delta Rescue

Desire and Ice

Rush

Spies and Stilettos

Wicked Hot

Hot Witness

Avenged

Never Surrender

Stand Alone Titles

Breath of Fire

Kill Shot

Catch Me If You Can

All About Eve

Paradise Disguised

Island Home

The Witching Hour

ALSO BY LOUIS SCOTT

Books by Liliana Hart and Scott Silverii

The Harley and Davidson Mystery Series

The Farmer's Slaughter

A Tisket a Casket

I Saw Mommy Killing Santa Claus

Get Your Murder Running

Deceased and Desist

Malice in Wonderland

Tequila Mockingbird

Gone With the Sin

ABOUT LILIANA HART

Liliana Hart is a New York Times, USAToday, and Publisher's Weekly bestselling author of more than sixty titles. After starting her first novel her freshman year of college, she immediately became addicted to writing and knew she'd found what she was meant to do with her life. She has no idea why she majored in music.

Since publishing in June 2011, Liliana has sold more than six-million books. All three of her series have made multiple appearances on the New York Times list.

Liliana can almost always be found at her computer writing, hauling five kids to various activities, or spending time with her husband. She calls Texas home.

If you enjoyed reading *this*, I would appreciate it if you would help others enjoy this book, too.

Lend it. This e-book is lending-enabled, so please, share it with a friend.

Recommend it. Please help other readers find this book by recommending it to friends, readers' groups and discussion boards.

Review it. Please tell other readers why you liked this book by reviewing. If you do write a review, please send me an email at lilianahartauthor@gmail.com, or visit me at http://www.lilianahart.com.

Connect with me online:
www.lilianahart.com
lilianahartauthor@gmail.com

facebook.com/LilianaHart

twitter.com/Liliana_Hart

instagram.com/LilianaHart

bookbub.com/authors/liliana-hart

ABOUT LOUIS SCOTT

Liliana's writing partner and husband, Scott blends over 25 years of heart-stopping policing Special Operations experience.

From deep in the heart of south Louisiana's Cajun Country, his action-packed writing style is seasoned by the Mardi Gras, hurricanes and crawfish étouffée.

Don't let the easy Creole smile fool you. The author served most of a highly decorated career in SOG buying dope, banging down doors, and busting bad guys.

Bringing characters to life based on those amazing experiences, Scott writes it like he lived it.

Lock and Load – Let's Roll.

Made in the USA
Middletown, DE
24 July 2021